GHOST DETECTORS ▸ VOLUME 1

LET THE SPECTER- DETECTING BEGIN!

BY
DOTTI ENDERLE

ILLUSTRATED BY
HOWARD MCWILLIAM

A special thanks to Melissa Markham —DE
For Rebecca —HM

The Lexile Framework for Reading® Lexile measure® 560L

Library of Congress Cataloging-in-Publication Data

Enderle, Dotti, 1954–

[Short stories. Selections]

Ghost detectors. Volume 1. Let the specter-detecting begin. Books 1–3 / by Dotti Enderle ; illustrated by Howard McWilliam. — First edition.

    pages   cm

Summary: In this first volume of three stories, ten-year-old best friends Malcom and Dandy thwart a practical-joking poltergeist, rid the Miller house of a ghost, and get to the bottom of some unusual paranormal activity in their elementary school.

ISBN 978-1-938063-28-2 (pbk. : alk. paper) — ISBN 978-1-938063-29-9 (electronic : alk. paper)

[1. Ghosts—Fiction. 2. Poltergeists—Fiction. 3. Supernatural—Fiction. I. McWilliam, Howard, 1977– illustrator. II. Title. III. Title: Let the specter-detecting begin.

PZ7.E69645Gf 2013

[Fic]—dc23

2013009115

Book design by Mighty Media Inc., Minneapolis, MN
Cover: Colleen Dolphin • Interior: Chris Long

Printed and Manufactured in the United States

Distributed by Publishers Group West

First edition

10 9 8 7 6 5 4 3 2 1

CONTENTS

BOOK 1

BOOK 2

BOOK 3

BOOK 1

IT CREEPS!

CHAPTER ONE

CON-FUSION

"So are you going to help me or not?" Malcolm asked his best friend, Dandy.

"Help you do what?" Dandy asked.

Malcolm narrowed his eyes like a real scientist. "The experiment I'm about to undertake in my lab. Are you going to help me?"

Dandy, whose real name was Daniel Dee, shrugged. "What kind of experiment?"

"Fusion," Malcolm answered. He was more eager to start than to explain.

Dandy scratched his head. "Fusion? Is that a real word?"

"I don't make up words," Malcolm said. "It's real."

"Will we have to sneak your sister's blow-dryer again?" Dandy asked, grinning.

Malcolm grinned back. "Maybe." He'd say anything to get Dandy's help, except make up words.

"Count me in!"

The boys bounced down the creaky steps into Malcolm's lab. Only it was really just the basement. Malcolm had shoved most everything stored there in the corner. On a long counter he kept his chemistry set, gizmos, and gadgets. The rotten-egg odor of last week's stink bomb still hung in the air.

"Hey, Malcolm. What are we going to fu— fu—uh—fusion?"

"Money," Malcolm said. "I have an idea that I think will help the economy."

Dandy scratched his head. "What's the economy?"

Dandy was a great best friend, but for a ten-year-old, he sure didn't know much. Malcolm sighed and patiently explained, "The economy has to do with earning and spending money."

Dandy picked his nose. "Doesn't sound very scientific."

"Wait 'til you see what I'm going to do. You know when something costs 97¢, and you have to dig in your pocket to find three quarters, two dimes, and two pennies?"

Dandy silently counted on his fingers to double-check.

"Well, most people hate having change jingling around in their pockets, so they have to give the clerk a dollar bill. Then they get back three pennies, which means they still have change jingling around in their pockets."

"Okay," Dandy said with a blank face.

"Well, why should change be separate? Wouldn't it be easier to buy something for 97¢ if the three quarters, two dimes, and two pennies were stuck together?"

Dandy nodded his head. "Oh yeah, I get it. Like with superglue?"

"No," Malcolm said, rolling his eyes. "We'll fuse it together. Then we'll present our idea to the government and win a medal from the president."

"Cool," Dandy said, picking his nose again. "So, do you want me to sneak your sister's blow-dryer?"

"No. I want you to loan me 97¢."

"Will I get it back?" Dandy asked.

3

Malcolm grinned. "All in one piece."

Dandy stood with his mouth wide open as Malcolm brought out his newest prize.

"Wow! Is that your mom's curling iron?" Dandy asked.

"No," Malcolm said. "It's my latest find. And close your mouth before you swallow a fly."

Dandy snapped his mouth shut—for a moment. "Where'd you find it?"

"In the back of one of my magazines," Malcolm answered. "It's made especially for fusing metal. When I turn it on, a red-hot laser will melt the money together. Are you ready?"

Malcolm stacked the coins on the counter, biggest on the bottom. He pointed his fusion wand, then flipped the switch.

No humming. No buzzing. No whirring. Just a click.

A thin stream of white light shone down on the coins.

"I thought the laser would be red," Dandy said.

"Shhhh," Malcolm snapped, giving Dandy a warning look. "It's hot. Like a white flame."

The boys stared at the money. Dandy sniffled.

"If it's that hot, wouldn't it burn a hole in the counter?"

Malcolm didn't answer, even though it was a good question. "Time's up," he finally said, clicking off the fusion wand.

Both boys inched slowly toward the table.

"Shouldn't there be smoke?" Dandy asked.

"Gosh, Dandy, don't you know anything? Lasers heat differently than fire."

They leaned forward, their noses just inches from the coins.

"Shouldn't it smell hot?" Dandy asked.

Malcolm reached his pointer finger toward the money. Slowly . . . slowly . . . slowly . . .

Dandy wiggled impatiently. "Well? Did the change . . . uh . . . change?"

Malcolm's finger touched the stack, and it came toppling down. He picked up one of the pennies. It wasn't even warm.

"What went wrong?" he muttered.

"Did you read the instructions?" Dandy asked.

"I couldn't. They were in Japanese."

Dandy picked up the fusion wand and turned it over. In tiny letters near the handle he read: *Mr. Laser Fun Flashlight—Galactic Toy Co.*

"I think I found the problem," he said, handing the flashlight to Malcolm.

Malcolm plunked himself down on an old beanbag chair. "Ripped off again! What do I do now?"

Dandy picked his nose and suggested, "Superglue?"

CHAPTER TWO

MAIL-ORDER MIRACLE

Malcolm dragged himself to breakfast the next morning. His pajamas were drooping and his hair was spiked from bed head.

His sister, Cocoa, and Grandma Eunice were already at the table. Cocoa was wearing blinding neon lip gloss that made her mouth look radioactive. Grandma Eunice just sat and ate her bran flakes and prunes. She was actually Malcolm's great-grandmother, and he thought she was probably older than electricity.

"Hey, coconut," Malcolm grunted.

"Mom! Malcolm called me coconut again!" Cocoa pouted.

Mom flipped a pancake. "Malcolm, don't call your sister 'coconut.'"

"It's your fault, Mom," Cocoa whined. "If

you'd given me a real name, I wouldn't have this problem."

"But sweetie," Mom said. "Your grandmother's name was Cocoa. Aren't you honored to be named after your grandmother?"

Malcolm gave Cocoa a wicked grin. "She could have named you after a different grandmother. How about we start calling you Eunice?"

Grandma Eunice looked up from her cereal and smiled. "That's nice."

Cocoa shot Malcolm a piercing look. "How about we call you nerd? Or do you prefer geek?"

Mom set the pancakes on the table. "I prefer quiet." She turned to Grandma Eunice, patted her shoulder, and adjusted the cereal spoon in her hand. "Can I get you something else to eat?" she asked.

Malcolm looked away. He hated the way everyone babied Grandma Eunice. They treated her more like a pet than a family member.

Grandma Eunice shook her head no, milk dripping down her chin.

Malcolm scarfed down his food and retreated to his lab to fiddle with his scientific gadgets.

At midmorning he looked up through the basement window and saw feet coming up the walk. He'd know those shoes anywhere. Mail Carrier Nancy.

Training—learn to take the howl out of moonlit nights.

SPECTER DETECTOR

Spooked by unseen spirits? Find them fast and easy with the new Ecto-Handheld-Automatic-Heat-Sensitive-Laser-Enhanced Specter Detector. Guaranteed to detect even the slyest of ghosts.

Batteries not included.

Learn ancient Egyptian magic in four short lessons

behind the

ENVIRO-BATT uses natural mat like mud, lem and water to p a light bulb, a w and activate a chip.

An amazing, science sc includes det so you can usual batteri coins, veget

Children Cl Hands-on Workshops cool experir workshop

Malcolm dashed to the mailbox and grabbed the stack of mail. He dropped the bills, flyers, and samples on the kitchen counter. Then, he ran back to his lab, holding his magazines.

This was the time of month Malcolm loved best. His magazines always arrived on the same day, just like Christmas presents. He sorted through them.

Junior Scientist. Weird Worlds. Beyond Belief. They were all here. But he rarely read the articles. Instead he'd jump to the ads in the back. That's where he found the cool inventions. He especially liked the ones that advertised as, *Originally developed in a secret government lab.*

Malcolm thumbed through the back of

Beyond Belief. Most of the ads were the same, month after month.

But a new ad caught Malcolm's eye. He practically drooled when he read it. Then, he circled it so he wouldn't forget it later.

Malcolm, who had a drawer full of batteries, leapt in the air. "Yes!"

His hands trembled as he stuffed the money into an envelope and licked it shut. He stuck on a stamp and ran to the corner mailbox. And then the waiting began.

CHAPTER THREE

THE ECTO-HANDHELD-AUTOMATIC-HEAT-SENSITIVE-LASER-ENHANCED SPECTER DETECTOR

Malcolm didn't do the things that other kids did during the summer. While they were swimming and playing ball, Malcolm watched science programs and monster movies and conducted experiments in his lab. But this summer, he mostly waited . . . and waited . . . and waited.

Every day he'd sit on the front stoop, watching for Mail Carrier Nancy to approach. And every day she'd say the same thing.

"Sorry, Malcolm. No packages." He hated those words.

Then finally, after two long weeks (which felt like two eternities to Malcolm), Mail Carrier Nancy walked up, wearing a grin bigger than her face.

"I believe this is for you," she said, handing Malcolm a heavily taped box.

Malcolm wanted to jump up and hug her, but he didn't think it would be appropriate. So instead, he thanked her and ran inside the house.

He rushed past Grandma Eunice as she sat watching her favorite soap opera. "Wheeeeeee!" she sang as he sped by.

He brushed by Cocoa, nearly knocking her down. "Hey, creep!" she shouted.

But Malcolm didn't hear either one. He was already flying down the basement steps, two at a time.

He knocked some magazines and empty cups off the counter and set the box down. He wished he had X-ray vision because he couldn't wait to see inside. He quickly took a pair of scissors and sliced through the label that said *Ecto Corporation*.

When he popped up the lid, an avalanche of white foam peanuts poured to his feet. After digging through what seemed like a million of those things, including the three that stuck to his arm, Malcolm found his prize! It was wrapped in a mile of Bubble Wrap. Oh well . . . it was better than getting a broken specter detector.

Malcolm unwound and unwound and unwound until—finally—he glimpsed it. The silver metal gadget shone like a trophy. It resembled a hand drill with three small bubbles on top, one red, one green, and one gold. It was the most beautiful thing Malcolm had ever seen.

He reached in to lift it out and was surprised at how heavy it was. This was no toy. On the left side of the handle was a small door for the batteries. On the right side was a switch. It looked easy enough. The switch was labeled Off—On—Detect.

Malcolm eyed the switch, butterflies thumping his belly. He took a deep breath and quickly flipped it on.

Nothing.

Then he remembered. *Batteries not included.*

He opened a drawer and selected two C batteries. They popped out three times before he got them installed. Then he tried the switch again. This time, he wasn't so nervous.

In the On position, the green light glowed, and the specter detector hummed. Malcolm was thrilled! He switched the gadget off and ran upstairs to the phone.

"Dandy, get over here quick. You've got to see this!"

CHAPTER FOUR

LIP-SYNCH

Malcolm stood in the front yard, waiting for Dandy. He impatiently rocked back and forth—one leg, then the other. Soon Dandy came thumping up the walk, taking his own sweet time.

"What do you want to show me?" he asked.

"It's in the lab. You gotta see it!"

When they walked into the living room, Grandma Eunice grinned at Dandy. "Hello, Alfred," she said.

Dandy looked back to make sure she wasn't talking to someone behind him. Then, he politely said, "My name is Daniel."

"That's nice," Grandma Eunice said, looking back at the TV.

The boys hurried past her and through the

kitchen. Malcolm grabbed a box of cheese crackers. Seeing ketchup stains on Dandy's shirt reminded him that he'd skipped lunch.

Before they reached the basement door, Malcolm heard music blaring so loud the walls rattled below. His stomach did a somersault.

He and Dandy rushed down the steps to an unforgivable sight. There was Cocoa, bopping to the music, snapping her fingers and mouthing the words. Her neon lip gloss had peeled into crusty clumps, looking a lot like the algae in Malcolm's fish tank.

Malcolm was thankful that Cocoa wasn't really singing. Her yowling was ten times worse than her dancing. He reached back and unplugged the CD player.

"Hey, nerd!" Cocoa hollered. "I need to practice for the lip-synch contest next week. This is important."

"You can practice," Malcolm said. "But not here. Out!"

"You don't own this basement!" she said. She planted her hands so firmly on her hips, her knuckles turned white.

"This is my lab. Get out!"

Dandy sat on the bottom step, picking his nose. "What did you want to show me?"

"Not yet," Malcolm said, staring his sister down.

"I'm not leaving," Cocoa said.

"Are too."

"Am not."

"Are too."

Dandy walked over and took the box of cheese crackers from Malcolm's hand. He removed his finger from his nose, popped open the lid, and dug in.

"Ewww, your friend is gross!" Cocoa cried.

"At least his boogers end up in his mouth and not all over his lips like yours," Malcolm said.

Cocoa smacked her lips together, causing the lip gloss to curl even more. "By the way, where's my blow-dryer?"

Dandy slowly backed away, looking at the floor. Cocoa gave him a suspicious look. "Where is it?"

"Why don't you go upstairs and look for it?" Malcolm suggested.

"I'm not leaving," she said, turning around and plugging the music back in.

"Fine," Malcolm said.

He headed over to his chemistry set. Dandy followed.

Malcolm took the Bubble Wrap from the specter detector and placed it on the floor behind the counter.

"What are you doing?" Dandy asked, spraying cracker crumbs.

"Getting rid of my sister." Malcolm took a clear beaker and filled it with vinegar. Then he poured in an entire bottle of blue 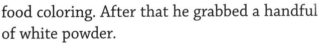 food coloring. After that he grabbed a handful of white powder.

Dandy took a step back and held his nose.

"Don't worry," Malcolm said. "It's not another stink bomb. It's baking soda. When I say now, you jump."

Malcolm put the beaker on the counter and waited until Cocoa was totally engrossed in her performance. Then, he tossed the baking soda into the beaker. Blue foam boiled up.

"Ahhhhhhhh!" Malcolm screamed, slapping both hands to his face.

Cocoa clicked off the CD player in a panic. "What is it?"

Malcolm's eyes grew wide with fake fear. "Ahhhhh! I put in the wrong chemical," Malcolm shouted. "The whole basement is going to blow. Run! Now!"

Dandy turned to run, but Malcolm grabbed his shoulder and pulled him back. "Now!"

The two boys jumped high, and came down right in the middle of the Bubble Wrap. It exploded in one earsplitting bang.

Cocoa screamed and flew up the stairs, barely touching a single step. Malcolm and Dandy burst into wild laughter as Malcolm ran up and locked the basement door.

Cocoa jiggled the knob, shouting, "I won't forget this, dweeb!"

Then Malcolm turned to Dandy. "Now I can show you the greatest gadget in the world."

CHAPTER FIVE

CHECK IT OUT!

"**B**e very careful," Malcolm said. He reached in the box and removed the specter detector with the care of a surgeon.

Dandy's eyes grew wide. "You're not going to point that thing at me, are you?"

"Why would I point it at you?" Malcolm said. "You're alive."

"Yeah, and I'd like to stay that way!"

"Dandy, do you have any idea what this is?" Malcolm's chest swelled with pride.

Dandy grinned. "Did you make something out of Cocoa's blow-dryer?"

"No. It's not a blow-dryer. It's my Ecto-Handheld-Automatic-Heat-Sensitive-Laser-Enhanced Specter Detector. It's for hunting ghosts!"

"Cool!" Dandy said. "Does it work?"

Malcolm shrugged. "I don't know. I haven't tried it out yet."

"Turn it on," Dandy said, reaching for the switch.

"Wait!" Malcolm hugged the specter detector close to keep Dandy's hands off. "I think this time we should read the instructions."

Dandy nodded. "Good idea."

Malcolm grabbed a small piece of paper out of the box. In bold letters across the top were the words, *WARNING: For Serious Ghost Hunters Only!*

No one was more serious about this than Malcolm. He kept reading.

WARNING: FOR SERIOUS GHOST HUNTERS ONLY!

Ecto-Handheld-Automatic-Heat-Sensitive-Laser-Enhanced Specter Detector

INSTRUCTION MANUAL

The Ecto-Handheld-Automatic-Heat-Sensitive-Laser-Enhanced Specter Detector is an essential tool for those committed to the study and understanding of spirit matter.

"What does that mean?" Dandy asked.

Malcolm shrugged. "It just means you have to be a serious ghost hunter."

Dandy rubbed his nose. "Then why don't they just say so?"

The specter detector will not fail to detect spirit matter or ecto activity where present.

"If there's a ghost around, it'll let you know," Malcolm translated.

1 *When the switch is in the On position, it will heat and activate the necessary sensors. The switch must be on for at least two minutes before detecting. A red light will come on as an indicator.*

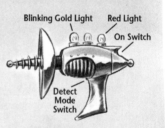

2 *Once the sensors are properly heated, the specter detector can then be switched to Detect mode. A blinking gold light and sound pulse will indicate Detect mode. One pulse per second indicates no activity. Three or more pulses per second indicates activity.*

"It has to warm up," Malcolm said.

Dandy looked at Malcolm like a kid lost in a department store. "Huh?"

"It'll make a noise," Malcolm said.

CAUTION: THIS ITEM IS NOT A TOY. PLEASE KEEP AWAY FROM NONPROFESSIONALS.

"We're not professionals," Dandy said.

Malcolm gave him a sour look. "Speak for yourself."

Dandy picked his nose and rubbed his finger on his shirt. "Okay, let's try it out."

"It's not that easy," Malcolm said. "We have to decide where we're going to try it."

"How about right here?" Dandy suggested.

Malcolm laughed out loud. "Here? You think there'd be ghosts around here? Come on, Dandy. The scariest thing around here is Grandma Eunice when she takes her teeth out at night."

"Then where are we going to find ghosts?" Dandy asked.

Malcolm dropped down on his bottom, right in the middle of the floor, and crossed his legs. He was careful to hold the specter detector with both hands. "That's what we have to figure out."

Dandy squatted down next to him and said, "How about the library?"

"Why the library?" Malcolm asked.

"I heard that sometimes the books drop off their shelves by themselves for no reason!"

"Dandy, that rumor was started by Mrs. Crutchmeyer. She's a lonely old librarian who will say anything to get people to come check out books."

Dandy just grunted in agreement. Malcolm suddenly had an idea.

"I've got it!" Malcolm jumped up and hurriedly put the specter detector in a drawer.

"What?" Dandy asked, still sitting.

"The McBleaky house!"

"No!" Dandy shot up off the floor. "No way!"

"Can you think of a better place?" Malcolm argued. "There's no doubt that it's haunted. Everyone knows it."

"And everyone stays away," Dandy added.

"Be a coward, I don't care," Malcolm said. "But I'm going there right now to check it out."

Malcolm headed toward the stairs, then looked back at Dandy. "Are you coming, or would you rather stay here and watch my sister hop around like a kangaroo with the chicken pox?"

Dandy stood for a moment considering. "Let's go," he finally said.

CHAPTER SIX

THE FREAKY MCBLEAKY HOUSE

Malcolm and Dandy snuck out the back and raced around to the front. They ran down the sidewalk, their sneakers pounding hard on the hot concrete.

After two blocks, Malcolm decided it was safe to slow down and walk, but he still hurried. He hadn't had this much fun since he invented a windshield wiper for his safety goggles with Cocoa's toothbrush.

The midday traffic hummed as the boys walked toward town. But instead of turning left on Main Street, they turned right and headed uphill, away from the buzz of the community.

Malcolm could see the McBleaky house, standing gray and gloomy up ahead. And the closer they got, the slower they walked, Dandy lagging several steps behind.

"Maybe I should wait here," Dandy said. "I wouldn't want to scare off any of the ghosts."

Malcolm gave him a look. "You couldn't scare a flea off a dog's behind. Keep walking."

Dandy crept slowly behind Malcolm, then shouted, "Wait!"

Malcolm nearly jumped out of his jeans. "Don't give me a heart attack like that! What's wrong?"

"You didn't bring the ghost detector."

Malcolm exhaled a barrel full of nervous air. "I know. We're just scoping the place out right now. Besides it's pointless to try and detect a ghost during the day. Don't you watch horror movies? They only come out at night."

"So when do you plan to look for ghosts?" Dandy asked.

Malcolm grinned. "Tonight."

Dandy turned a sickly shade of white. "A-alone?"

"Don't be silly," Malcolm said. "You're spending the night tonight."

Dandy's face drooped. "Tonight?"

"Don't be such a baby. Let's go."

Malcolm and Dandy walked up to the crumbling picket fence. It was an awesome sight. Even in the middle of summer, the trees looked dead and mossy. The weeds were taller than the first floor windows, and the second story of the house sagged. The top windows reminded Malcolm of sleepy eyes, waiting and watching.

Malcolm stepped onto the creaky McBleaky porch. He grinned.

"Dandy," he whispered to his jittery friend, "a creaky porch is a definite sign of a haunted house."

A cottony cobweb guarded the front door. "Bingo," Malcolm said. "Another sure sign."

And when he opened the squeaky McBleaky door, he knew he couldn't have picked a better place. Malcolm was sure that nothing was living here. But just as they were about to step in, two hands grabbed their shoulders. Malcolm and Dandy whipped around with a scream.

"Ahhhhhhhhhhh!" A most hideous monster stood inches away!

"I'm going to tell Mom you came here," Cocoa said, pursing her lips.

It took Malcolm a few seconds to catch his breath. "You followed us!"

"That's right," Cocoa said. "I told you I'd pay you back. Now you're in big trouble, mister."

"Well, if I'm in trouble then so are you. You're here too." Malcolm gave Cocoa a smug grin.

"Not if I tell Mom that I followed you because I knew you were up to something," Cocoa said.

"And I'll tell Mom that you don't mind your own business," Malcolm argued.

Cocoa pressed her fists to her hips. "I'll tell Mom that you could have been killed out here, and I was only doing it for your own good."

"I'll tell Mom that I saw you kissing Carson O'Donnell behind the school last week."

Cocoa gasped and covered her mouth. "You didn't see that," she whispered.

"Yes, I did," Malcolm said. "And you're just lucky I haven't told Mom before now."

Cocoa stood up tall and raised her nose in the air. "Fine. I won't say anything if you won't."

"Fine," Malcolm said. "Now go away."

Cocoa stepped off the rickety porch and pushed through the tall weeds. She looked back and yelled, "But you better bring back my blow-dryer!"

Once she was gone, Dandy shook his head. "Your sister is weird."

Malcolm nodded. "But not as weird as this old house. It's perfect. We're definitely coming back tonight."

CHAPTER SEVEN

GRANNY-SITTING

Malcolm sat with his family at dinner that evening, but his mind was on ghost detecting. Everyone was unusually quiet. Dad had the TV blaring from the living room so he could hear the six o'clock news. Malcolm saw his chance to launch Step One of his ghost-hunting plan.

"Mom, can Dandy spend the night?"

"Of course," Mom said. "He can keep you company while you watch Grandma Eunice."

The spaghetti in Malcolm's mouth suddenly tasted like lead. "I'm watching Grandma Eunice tonight?"

"It's just for a few hours," Mom said.

"Why can't Cocoa watch her?"

Mom laid down her fork. "Because Cocoa is going with me."

"Why can't I go?" Malcolm asked. He didn't really want to go anywhere with them, but he wanted to protest.

Mom sighed and lifted her fork again. "You can go if you think you'll enjoy shopping for Cocoa's new dress."

Cocoa wrinkled her nose and smirked at him.

Malcolm wouldn't give up. "Why can't Dad watch Grandma?"

"Bowling night," Dad said, shoveling spaghetti into his mouth.

Malcolm sank in his chair. It was useless. He looked over at Grandma Eunice, who didn't seem to notice they were talking about her. She had a large napkin tucked in her collar, and there appeared to be more spaghetti on her chin and fingers than on her plate.

He spoke to her in a defeated voice. "I'm staying with you tonight, Grandma Eunice."

She gave him a tomatoey grin. "That's nice."

His plan to sneak back to the McBleaky house might not work after all.

That evening, Grandma Eunice sat on the edge of the sofa, watching an old black-and-

white TV show. Dandy was lying on the floor, using Cocoa's blow-dryer to balance a ping-pong ball. The ball floated on the steady jet of warm air—a trick Malcolm had shown him a few weeks ago.

Malcolm was stretched out on the other end of the couch, tapping the toes of his sneakers together out of pure boredom. He looked at

his watch. Eight thirty. What time did the mall close, anyway? Knowing Mom and Cocoa, they'd stop off for a soda or ice cream afterward. And Dad wouldn't be home until after eleven o'clock.

Dandy shut off the blow-dryer and let the ping-pong ball drop. It dribbled across the floor, then rolled into the corner. "When can we go?" he asked.

Malcolm sat up. "We may not be able to go at all tonight. I don't think I can sneak out if it's very late."

Grandma Eunice threw her head back and laughed at something on TV.

"Maybe we shouldn't be talking about this in front of your great-grandmother," Dandy whispered, pointing her way.

"It's okay," Malcolm said. "She doesn't know what's going on."

"Oh well," Dandy said. "I don't want to go to that house at night anyway. That place was scary enough in the daylight."

"I just have to go," Malcolm said. "And I'm taking my camera. If my specter detector can really detect a ghost, I might be able to capture it on film."

Grandma Eunice laughed again, this time slapping her leg. A bit of drool rolled down the corner of her face.

"Maybe there's another house we could test it out on," Dandy suggested.

Malcolm shook his head furiously. "No, it has to be the McBleaky house!"

Suddenly the television shut off. Malcolm

36

looked over at Grandma Eunice. She sat with the remote still extended in her hand. Her face looked young and bright, and her eyes were lit like someone half her age. "You don't want to go there," she said.

Malcolm leaned toward her and looked her in the eyes. "Grandma?"

"You don't want to go to the McBleaky house," Grandma Eunice warned. "It's not fit for any living soul, especially little boys."

Malcolm couldn't believe it. His great-grandmother had some wits about her after all. "How do you know about the McBleaky house?" he asked, still not convinced she was totally all there.

"Because I knew Old Man McBleaky himself. And I know what happened in that house."

"What?" Malcolm and Dandy asked, huddling together.

Grandma Eunice moved in closer to the boys. "It all started about 80 years ago . . ."

CHAPTER EIGHT

THE TALE

Malcolm and Dandy leaned toward Grandma Eunice. Her eyes looked distant. Not like before when she was in another world, but like she was remembering.

She continued, "The McBleakys built that house in the 1920s. They had two boys, Howard and Herbert. Howard was the serious one, always worried about school and his paper route. Herbert was the joker. He made Howard's life miserable, constantly putting dead flies in his ice cubes or fishing string across the bottom of his doorway. Howard hated it. He swore he'd get Herbert back one day.

"Their parents were killed when they were young men. Their mother was struck by lightning while hanging out the wash, and their dad caught it in a tractor accident. Both within just a couple of months of each other.

"The boys were left alone in that house, but they were old enough to look after themselves. Everyone thought that with the parents gone Herbert would straighten up and get serious. No sir. He kept right on pulling those awful jokes on his brother.

"But then Herbert up and kicked the bucket himself. No one ever knew the true cause of his death. But Neb Fuller, the barber, overheard Howard whispering at the funeral, 'Guess I got the last laugh.'

"Within a few days, Howard started coming into town, his eyes all red and bloodshot, his face weary and tired. 'What's wrong, Howard?' people would ask. He'd just lift his heavy head and say, 'Can't sleep.'

"Then he started aging real fast. He became bitter and frail. He'd hobble around town shaking his fist and hollering at folks. People stayed out of his way.

"One day, I saw a crowd by the fence of the McBleaky house. An ambulance was parked in front, and two men in white coats were hauling

Howard out the door. He was dressed in nothing but his boxer shorts. He was screaming at the top of his lungs, 'I can't take it anymore! He's still playing tricks on me!' It was a pitiful sight.

"After that, no one's been able to stay in that house. Not one living soul. Herbert's ghost is still there, and he's as loony as ever. So I suggest you and your friend here find another place to try out your ghost gadget."

Malcolm blinked. Was he dreaming?

"Grandma Eunice, I can't believe it. You still have all your marbles!"

"Yes, sir," she said, tapping a crooked finger to her head. "They're all right here."

"Then why are you always pretending to be on Planet Weird?"

Grandma Eunice laughed. "I act the way I'm treated. I tried to convince your mother a long time ago that I'm sane. But for some reason, she and everyone else wants to treat me like I'm one banana short of a bunch. I just go along with it to make them happy. Besides, it keeps me from having to take a turn doing the dishes."

Malcolm couldn't resist. He reached over and gave Grandma Eunice a hug.

"Now," she said, "why don't you and Alfred here go on to your laboratory and find something fun to do? I'm okay."

Malcolm and Dandy hopped up and headed out of the room.

"And Malcolm, honey," Grandma Eunice called out, "try not to talk about me while I'm in the room."

When he looked back, she winked and smiled.

CHAPTER NINE

SNEAKING OUT— SNEAKING IN

Grandma Eunice's story was meant as a warning. But, it just confirmed what Malcolm already knew. The McBleaky house was definitely haunted!

Malcolm's luck was running high. His mom and sister came home early, and Mom went straight to bed, complaining of a headache.

The two boys took their sleeping bags to the basement, claiming they'd sleep down in the lab. Malcolm locked the basement door and pulled out a backpack he'd packed that afternoon.

"What's in there?" Dandy asked.

"Everything we'll need to detect a ghost," Malcolm answered.

"Don't we just need the specter detector?"

Malcolm rolled his eyes. "And a flashlight and a tape recorder and a camera."

"What about a snack?"

"Dandy, honestly, why would we need a snack?"

"In case we get hungry."

Malcolm couldn't believe it. Dandy was serious. "We're not going to get hungry. We won't be there long enough to get hungry! And if you happen to get hungry, maybe the ghost will be polite and offer you something to eat."

Dandy shrugged. "Okay."

Malcolm opened the skinny basement window, climbed up on a chair and slithered out. He looked back in at Dandy. "You're not going to chicken out, are you?"

Dandy hopped up on the chair. "I'm right behind you."

And Dandy stayed right behind Malcolm the whole way. About three feet back, dragging the soles of his sneakers and biting his fingernails.

Malcolm had the jitters, too. Partly from fear, partly from excitement. He had to be brave. This was his one shot at fame. If he could detect a ghost, record it, and capture it on film, he'd be written up in every major newspaper in the country . . . make that in the world! He wished he'd brought the video camera.

The McBleaky house stood just ahead of them, like a black hole ready to suck them in. Malcolm could hear Dandy's teeth chattering. Once they were hidden by the towering weeds, Malcolm pulled out the flashlight and clicked it on. A circle of white light hit the porch, and Malcolm saw an army of tiny critters skittering into the shadows.

Dandy gulped loudly when they reached the door. "Are you sure we should go in there? That's trespassing."

"Who would come and arrest us?" Malcolm asked. "Even the cops are afraid of this place."

Dandy grabbed Malcolm's shoulder. "Shouldn't that tell you something? If cops are afraid, then what are a couple of dumb kids like us doing here?"

Malcolm set the backpack down and pulled out his specter detector. "This," he said with pride. "Now, do as I say, and don't be a baby."

The door opened easily. *Eeeeeeeeek.*

Malcolm stepped in, turned on the specter detector, then pointed the flashlight at his watch. "It's warming up."

Dandy still had a death grip on Malcolm's shoulder. "I have to use the bathroom."

"No, you don't," Malcolm said, not taking his eyes off his watch. "Two minutes, that's all it'll take."

The house was still and quiet. The only noises were the ticking of Malcolm's watch and Dandy's ragged breathing. They waited. *Tick. Tick. Tick.*

Something moved in the corner. Malcolm whipped the flashlight around and stabbed the darkness. A mouse scurried across and disappeared into a crack.

Only one minute. He counted the seconds silently, *one Frankenstein, two Frankenstein, three Frankenstein.* Dandy's grip had become a serious squeeze, but in less than a minute they'd be on the move.

When the second hand hit the two minute

mark, Malcolm reached for the switch. "You ready?" he asked Dandy.

Dandy stood paralyzed. Malcolm figured he wasn't going to get an answer, and flipped the specter detector to Detect. The green light flashed off, and the gold light flashed on. But only for a second. The light then blinked off and on with a steady *bleep—bleep—bleep*.

"Not much activity right now," Malcolm said, turning to look back at Dandy. Dandy's eyes were wide-open. His lips looked blue, even in the brassy hue of the flicking specter detector light.

"Just stick with me," Malcolm said, although he figured Dandy wasn't thinking for a second of venturing off on his own. Malcolm took slow baby steps, tiptoeing across the floor, Dandy's hand still gripping him. Dandy never lifted his feet. He skated behind Malcolm, without a breath.

Malcolm kept the flashlight pointed in his left hand, the detector in his right. As they approached the fireplace, two eyes peered down at them.

"What?" Malcolm sputtered, whipping the light toward the mantle. Just an ugly giant moose head, hung up like a trophy. Malcolm took a moment to breathe and gather everything that was just scared out of him.

When they reached a spiral staircase, Malcolm whispered to Dandy, "Reach in my backpack and turn on the tape recorder. Then pull out the camera and turn on the flash."

Dandy never said a word. He obeyed Malcolm, but took forever doing it because of his nervous fumbling. And even though Malcolm tried to stand still, the light from the flashlight danced all over the foot of the staircase. But Malcolm was patient. He had to be. He hadn't told Dandy, but he'd stay here all night if he had to.

As it turned out, he didn't have to wait long. Like a fisherman hoping for a catch, Malcolm had a bite. The gold light blinked faster.

Bleep-bleep-bleep-bleep-bleep.

Both boys froze, staring down at the rapid signal. The beam from the flashlight bent and flickered. Then something brushed the hairs on Malcolm's neck. A voice, as thin as the wind, whispered in Malcolm's ear.

"It creeeeeeeeps."

CHAPTER TEN

IT CREEPS!

Malcolm's guts turned to jelly. Fear spread through him, tingling from head to toe. The specter detector kept on detecting.

Bleep-bleep-bleep-bleep-bleep.

Malcolm turned to see Dandy standing like a zombie. His lips were purple and his eyes hollow.

"Run, Dandy!" Malcolm screamed. He turned and ran for the front door. He tugged and tugged, but the door was bolted shut.

Malcolm slumped against the door. He had to think . . . he had to plan . . . he had to decide what to do next. He'd been so preoccupied with detecting a ghost, he never stopped to think about what he'd do when he found one.

The specter detector sped up. *Bleep-bleep-bleep-bleep-bleep-bleep!*

The kitchen door was just across the room. If he could make it there, he could blast through and rush out the back. But as he darted toward it, something caught his hair and jerked him back. He landed splat on his bottom. The flashlight crashed to the floor and everything went black.

"It creeeeeeeeps. It creeeeeeeeps."

"Yeow!" Malcolm came off the floor faster than a cat on hot sand. He sprinted toward the kitchen, bumping into Dandy, who still stood petrified. Just as Malcolm reached the kitchen door, it swung open, but before he entered, it slammed shut again . . . smashing him right in the face.

He staggered backward, stars falling in front of his face. The dark room went in and out of focus. But Malcolm could still hear the specter detector beeping away, even faster now.

Bleep-bleep-bleep-bleep-bleep-bleep-bleep-bleep! In his daze, he heard that wispy voice. "It creeeeeeeeps. It creeeeeeeeps."

He fell into the kitchen and looked around. No back door! Was this a joke? He crawled under a large rusty sink. He had to collect his thoughts, or at least the ones that hadn't been whacked out of him by the kitchen door.

He took a deep breath. *Think! Think!* Now his specter detector bleeped faster than a baseball card on bicycle spokes.

Bleepbleepbleepbleepbleepbleepbleepbleepbleep! Something grabbed Malcolm's nose, tweaking it hard. "It creeeeeeeeps. It creeeeeeeeps."

"Ouch!" Malcolm shot out from behind the sink and pushed through the kitchen door again. "Dandy!" he screamed. Dandy just stood there, not even blinking.

Malcolm hid under the stairs. It was just an inky black hole, with the exception of the gold light from the specter detector, now bleeping so fast, it generated one continuous beam. *Bleeeeeeeeeeeeeeeeeeeeeeeeeeeep!* Malcolm knew what that meant.

"It creeeeeeeeps. It creeeeeeeeps."

He jumped out from under the stairs and tried to run, but someone or something had knotted his shoelaces. He tripped and fell forward. The specter detector dropped from his hands and skittered across the floor.

Malcolm crawled on his elbows and belly,

slithering like a snake. In a panic, he grabbed the gadget and tried flipping the switch off. It was jammed.

Bleeeeeeeeeeeeeeeeeeeeeeeeeep!

He jiggled it and tugged at it.

Bleeeeeeeeeeeeeeeeeeeeeeeeeep!

He banged it on the floor.

Bleeeeeeeeeeeeeeeeeeeeeeeeeep!

Then in a moment of desperation, he opened the little door and popped out the batteries.

Bleeeeeeeeeeeeeeeeeeeeeeeeeep!

Malcolm stared wildly at the specter detector. Was he losing his mind?

Bleeeeeeeeeeeeeeeeeeeeeeeeeeeep!

"It creeeeeeeps. It creeeeeeeeps."

Malcolm hung his head and whimpered. He didn't need his specter detector. What he had come to find had found him.

"It creeeeeeeps. It creeeeeeeeps."

Malcolm couldn't take it anymore. "What creeps! What creeps!"

"YOUR UNDERWEAR!"

Suddenly something lifted Malcolm in the air by the elastic waistband of his drawers. Yanked higher and higher. He thought he'd split in two. Then it hooked him on one pointed antler of the moose head over the fireplace. And there Malcolm hung, like a wet sock.

The specter detector went silent. The light dimmed and disappeared. And just as Malcolm's breathing slowed, a brilliant flash filled the room. A giant spot appeared before his eyes.

"What was that?" he yelled.

Dandy flipped on the flashlight and aimed it at Malcolm's face. "Didn't you want me to take a picture?"

CHAPTER ELEVEN

WINDING DOWN

"**H**ow'd you get up there?" Dandy asked.

Malcolm shook his head. "You didn't see? You didn't hear?"

Dandy shrugged, then he looked around until he found an old broom to help get Malcolm loose from the moose.

Malcolm couldn't believe his underwear could stretch that far! He wondered if any was left covering his behind. With the help of the broom handle, he managed to pluck the elastic free and fall to the ground.

"Let's go!" he yelled.

After the boys snatched up their things, including the specter detector, Dandy ran for the front door.

"It's locked," Malcolm said. "We'll have to

find another exit." But Dandy turned the handle and the door opened with a gentle squeak.

Wasting no time, they raced out the door, scampered over the rickety porch, trudged through the weedy walkway, and jumped the wobbly picket fence. They didn't stop until they reached Malcolm's front yard, where they collapsed on the lawn, gasping and groaning.

"What were we running away from?" Dandy asked.

Malcolm buried his face in this hands. "I can't believe you didn't see it or hear it."

"I saw the light on the ghost detector blinking," Dandy said. "It blinked and blinked and blinked . . ." Dandy's eyelids relaxed and he stared off in a trance.

"It must have hypnotized you!" Malcolm said. He snapped his fingers in front of Dandy's eyes to wake him up.

"Anyway," Dandy continued, "the next thing I knew, you were hanging from that moose."

Malcolm stood up and looked at his bottom. The elastic of his underwear was drooping over his pants. "Let's go in," he said.

Dandy stared off down the street. "All this ghost hunting has made me tired. I think I'll go home."

Malcolm watched as Dandy drifted down
the sidewalk like someone sleepwalking. He
disappeared around the corner.

Malcolm still had the jitters when he slipped
into his house. Even though Dandy had gone,
he still had the feeling he wasn't alone. He was
being watched. Had someone or something
followed him home?

He moved quietly to his lab to put away his
equipment. As he reached the basement door,
he met with another shock. Cocoa was blocking
the way, hands on her hips, and her mouth tight
as a wire.

"Where is it?" she growled.

"What?"

"Where is my blow-dryer?"

Malcolm's shoulders sank. He was in no
mood to deal with her tonight. "I'll get it in the
morning," he said.

"Look at my hair! It looks like a heap of
spaghetti. I need my blow-dryer! Get it tonight!"

She screamed so hard that Malcolm could see
clear down her throat. "Okay, okay," he said. "I'll
put it in your bathroom."

Cocoa stormed away, slamming her bedroom
door.

The excitement of the evening wore off, and Malcolm's feet suddenly felt like bricks. He trudged down the stairs and put his equipment away. He found Cocoa's blow-dryer where Dandy had hidden it. He looked at it for a moment, then pulled out his specter detector.

Hmmmmm . . . An evil thought crossed his mind. Herbert McBleaky wasn't the only practical joker in town. He slipped in and out of Cocoa's bathroom with a devilish grin.

CHAPTER TWELVE
PAYBACK

Malcolm had a night full of weird dreams where he was chased by ghosts, his sister, and a large moose. He could barely tell one from the other. But the sun, shining on his face, told him it was time to get up and start the day.

He sat down to his usual bowl of cereal. Everything seemed unusually white and transparent this morning. Malcolm figured it was just a trick of the light.

Mom stood at the stove, making eggs for Dad. Dad sat at the end of the table, reading the newspaper. And Grandma Eunice sat eating her prunes. It appeared to be a normal summer morning.

Grandma looked shriveled and small staring at the back of the newspaper. Then Malcolm noticed the light in her eyes. She wasn't staring off . . . she was reading the article! She turned to Malcolm and winked, then went back to her reading. Malcolm couldn't help but smile.

Malcolm poured his milk and dug into his breakfast. Before he got the spoon to his mouth, a bloodcurdling scream echoed down the hall from the bathroom.

Dad spilled his coffee. Mom dropped a plate. Grandma Eunice dribbled prune juice down her chin. And a moment later, Cocoa came rushing through the kitchen holding the specter detector, her wet hair slapping against her face as she ran past the table.

Malcolm couldn't see what was chasing her, but he was pretty sure it was the ghost that had followed him home last night.

Cocoa raced about, jumping and grabbing her bottom like someone was popping her with a towel.

Mom and Dad ran after her. Malcolm just sat and ate his cereal. He guessed that the specter detector would fix Cocoa's spaghetti hair problem. After this, it should be standing straight up!

Payback was fun, but there was more work to do.

Malcolm got dressed, then hurried down the street to the nearest mailbox. It was time to send off for another weird gadget. *The Ecto-Handheld-Automatic-Heat-Sensitive-Laser-Enhanced Ghost Zapper. Guaranteed to zap the peskiest of ghosts. *Batteries not included.*

BOOK 2

I'M GONNA GET YOU!

WAIT ... WAIT ... WAIT

Malcolm waited on his front porch steps. He craned his neck to the right, looking as far down the street as possible.

His best friend, Dandy, sat next to him. Dandy wiggled his finger in his ear like he was trying to loosen something.

"Where is she?" Malcolm said.

"What?" Dandy asked.

"I've been waiting for weeks, and today is finally the day. I can't believe she's late." Malcolm got up and started to pace in front of the porch.

"What?" Dandy repeated.

Malcolm sighed and then removed Dandy's finger from his ear. "She's never this late."

Dandy shrugged. "Oh. Well, maybe she had an emergency."

Malcolm thought about that. "What kind of emergency would a mail carrier have?"

"Maybe she had to deliver a baby." Dandy put his finger back into his ear and jiggled it some more.

"She's a mail carrier, Dandy, not a stork!"

Malcolm sat back down and tapped his foot impatiently. He had already used his Ecto-Handheld-Automatic-Heat-Sensitive-Laser-Enhanced Specter Detector. It worked well. Too well!

Malcolm cringed. He still had nightmares about the major wedgie that prankster ghost, Herbert McBleaky, had given him.

After that experience, Malcolm had decided that it was no use detecting a ghost if you couldn't get rid of it. So Malcolm had ordered an Ecto-Handheld-Automatic-Heat-Sensitive-Laser-Enhanced Ghost Zapper. And he intended to use it!

Dandy looked at his fingers, then burrowed into his other ear. "You never told me the plan. Are we going after Herbert McBleaky?"

"Naw. I think we should detect a tamer ghost first and use the zapper on him."

"But where are we going to find a tamer ghost?"

"There are ghosts everywhere," Malcolm told him. "We'll just go on a ghost hunt."

Dandy's face brightened. "Yeah! Like a treasure hunt!" Then he paused. "Except we'd find something scary instead of something fun."

"No one said ghost detecting would be fun," Malcolm said. "It's certainly not for the weak of heart." Although as Malcolm said it, he wasn't so sure he was really all that brave.

Dandy gave him a blank stare. It was the same look he gave his mom when she'd ask if he'd cleaned his room. "If it isn't fun, then why are we even doing it?"

Didn't Dandy understand anything? "For the greater good," Malcolm replied. "We'll rid the world of all the stray ghosts. I mean, think about it. They're just hanging out, making houses uninhabitable."

Dandy gave him that blank look again.

"*Uninhabitable* means no one can live there," Malcolm informed him.

"Oh," Dandy said, still drilling into his ear.

Malcolm squinted his eyes, looking down

the street for Mail Carrier Nancy. He began to wonder if she really did have an emergency.

Or maybe she called in sick, and her replacement used a different route. He tapped his foot some more. He was close to jumping up and running down the street to look for her.

Just when he thought he might actually fly out of his own skin, he saw her turn the corner. She was pulling her mail cart and zigzagging from house to house.

Dandy took his finger out of his ear, smelled it, then wiped it on his Iron Man T-shirt. Malcolm and Dandy both stood as Mail Carrier Nancy approached, a smile beaming from her face.

"I have a package for you," she told Malcolm.

"Yes!" he cheered, meeting her halfway. She dug into the cart. Still wearing a smile, she came up with the package and a few other letters for Malcolm's family.

Her look quickly changed as she glanced behind Malcolm. She now shuddered in terror. Her eyes grew large and her mouth formed a perfect O.

Malcolm knew of only one creature that could put that look of horror on a person's face. He had a feeling that what stood behind him was the most terrifying thing on Earth.

CHAPTER TWO

BLACKMAIL

A hand clamped down on Malcolm's shoulder and he quickly spun around. His sister, Cocoa, stood there sneering. It was exactly as he'd feared.

"What'd you do with it?" she barked. She wore electric blue eye shadow and lip gloss so orange it reminded Malcolm of a hazard sign. Some had smeared onto her front teeth. She dug her plum purple fingernails into Malcolm's collarbone.

Malcolm grew pale. "Go away."

"Not until you tell me what you did with it!" Cocoa leaned so close he could smell the tuna fish sandwich still lingering on her breath.

"Just tell her," Dandy begged. He slowly backed away, like he might scream and sprint off at any moment.

"I don't even know what she's talking about," Malcolm said.

Cocoa squinted at him. "I'm talking about my iPod, loser. I know you took it."

True, Malcolm had snuck her iPod out of her room. He'd heard of people picking up spirit messages on walkie-talkies and in TV static. Ghosts liked communicating through electronics. He figured if Cocoa could download music on it, then maybe he could rig it to download ghost voices.

So, he'd simply converted her iPod into an apparition-receiving device. Once it was perfected, he'd planned to call it *iHaunts – Voices from Beyond*.

"Give it back, dweeb!" Cocoa demanded.

"Uh-hum." Mail Carrier Nancy cleared her throat. "Here's your mail."

Malcolm reached for it, but Cocoa was quicker. She snatched it away so fast, Malcolm felt like he was in a time warp.

"Hey!" he cried as Cocoa headed back up the sidewalk. "That's my package!"

"Yeah? You can have it when I get my iPod back!" She gave him a sneer that could only be seen in a carnival spook house. Even Mail Carrier Nancy cringed.

"Do something," Malcolm told Dandy.

Dandy stuck his finger back in his ear. "She's your sister."

Mail Carrier Nancy clutched her cart. "Good luck, boys." She hurried away.

"I want my package!" Malcolm yelled as he stormed into the house. Dandy followed, doing a double step to catch up.

"You know the deal," Cocoa said, slamming and locking her bedroom door.

Malcolm wasn't going to take this. He'd dealt with Cocoa way too many times to let this one slide. He'd been waiting more than six weeks for that package! So he did the one thing he knew he had to do. "MOM!"

Malcolm stomped into the kitchen where his mother sat, making a grocery list. Just as he started to protest, she looked up, relief in her eyes.

"Malcolm, would you please get your toy away from Grandma Eunice? She's driving me crazy."

Grandma Eunice was actually Malcolm's

great-grandmother. She'd been living with them as long as he could remember.

Just as his mother spoke, Grandma Eunice came creaking into the kitchen in her wheelchair. She held the Ecto-Handheld-Automatic-Heat-Sensitive-Laser-Enhanced

Specter Detector in her hand. She was swinging it back and forth, aiming it at nothing.

"Where are you, you son of a gun?" she called. She gazed intensely at the air in the room.

"Who are you looking for?" Malcolm asked.

"Who do you think?" she said. "Your great-grandpa Bertram."

"Grandma Eunice," Mom sighed. "Grandpa Bertram died in 1977."

"But he's still haunting me. He used to bring me jellybeans!" She swung around, aiming the ghost detector into the dining room. "Bertram! I want more jellybeans!"

"Malcolm," Mom said, trying to stay patient, "please take your toy back to the basement."

Malcolm gestured for Grandma Eunice to give it up. "Hand it over, Grandma. You're not even using it right."

She gave it to Dandy instead. "Here, Alfred," she whined. "No one around here plays fair."

Malcolm knew that Mom wasn't up for another crisis. He'd have to deal with Cocoa himself.

"Come on, Dandy." The boys headed for Cocoa's bedroom.

"Dude," Dandy said, "your family is bonkers."

Malcolm looked at Dandy, who had one finger in his ear and the other up his nose.

"Yeah," he agreed. Down the hall he could hear Grandma Eunice shout, "Bertram, I want my jellybeans!"

CHAPTER THREE

SUPERWEAPON

Malcolm handed Cocoa her iPod, and she slapped the package into his chest.

"Now go away!" she screamed, slamming the door. Malcolm was more than happy to leave.

He and Dandy hurried down to his lab in the basement. His heart was pumping faster again. The excitement had returned.

"Do you have any idea how high tech this is?" Malcolm asked Dandy as he ripped the tape off the box.

Dandy didn't answer. He just stood rubbing his belly, waiting to see what was inside.

Even though the box was big, Malcolm could see that it was mostly filled with Bubble Wrap. He began unwrapping it. The unwinding seemed to take forever. Finally, he had it in his hand.

His very own Ecto-Handheld-Automatic-Heat-Sensitive-Laser-Enhanced Ghost Zapper.

"Uh . . . that's it?" Dandy asked. They both stared at the object Malcolm held.

Dandy scratched his nose. "Shouldn't it be bigger?"

Malcolm wondered the same thing. The ad in the back of *Worlds Beyond* magazine made it look like a megamachine. But it looked more like an aerosol can with a trigger. Even the laser was hidden.

"It looks like my mom's hairspray," Dandy added.

Malcolm reached back into the box and pulled out the instructions. He read them out loud.

Your Ecto-Handheld-Automatic-Heat-Sensitive-Laser-Enhanced Ghost Zapper is the perfect companion to the Ecto-Handheld-Automatic-Heat-Sensitive-Laser-Enhanced Specter Detector. Once a ghost has been detected, shake well, aim, and squeeze the trigger.

CAUTION: USE ONLY AS DIRECTED.

"That seems easy enough," Dandy said. "Are we going on a ghost hunt now?"

Malcolm shrugged. He was truly disappointed. All this time he'd pictured himself lugging a superweapon that would disintegrate any ghost in his path. This thing looked more like something he'd use to spray graffiti on them. But still, it must work. There was only one way to find out.

"Yeah," Malcolm said, "I think we might need to search out a ghost . . . you know . . . to test it."

Dandy's face split into a huge grin, but then he tried to look serious. "Where do we start?"

"I think we should just keep the ghost detector on all the time," Malcolm said. "Let the ghosts find us."

"Like your great-grandpa?" Dandy asked with a straight face.

"What? No!" Malcolm said. "Grandma Eunice is just being silly."

"But you never know. After all, I was there too. I know she isn't batty," Dandy whispered, looking around the room.

Malcolm switched the ghost detector to On. Once it warmed up, he flipped it to Detect. They both looked around, waiting.

Finally Malcolm said, "See? No Grandpa

Bertram. Besides, I think I could sense if my own house was haunted."

That's when the basement door flew open with a bang. Cocoa came stomping down the stairs. "Hey creep, aren't you forgetting something?"

Malcolm rolled his eyes. "Yeah, I forgot to lock the door!"

"You forgot about dogsitting!"

Yikes! Malcolm had been worrying so much about his package arriving that he'd forgotten he'd promised to feed the Millers' dogs while they were on vacation. And they'd left last night.

"Can't you do it?" Malcolm asked Cocoa.

"And have a sneezing fit? You know I'm allergic to dogs."

Malcolm remembered Cocoa's last sneezing fit. Her nose turned purple and her pea green eye shadow ran down to her cheeks, mixing with her maroon blush. She'd looked like a clown on meltdown. Yuck!

"Fine," Malcolm said. "I'm going." He tucked his ghost detector into the waistband of his jeans. Then he and Dandy headed out.

CHAPTER FOUR

DOG**S**ITTING

Malcolm squinted against the afternoon sun as he and Dandy headed down the sidewalk. He couldn't believe he'd forgotten to feed the dogs.

Dandy was humming. Malcolm had no idea what tune it was though. It sounded like a cross between "Pop Goes the Weasel" and the theme from *Star Trek*.

"So we're just going to dump some food in their bowls then go ghost hunting, right?" Dandy asked.

"It's not just feeding them," Malcolm said. "It's dogsitting. I have to pet them and play with them. You know, make sure they're not lonely."

Dandy looked at him like it was the first day of school. "How long will that take?"

Malcolm sighed. "I don't know. Until the dogs are tired of us, I guess."

"And you have to do this for how long?"

"Just for a week."

Dogsitting wasn't new to Malcolm. He'd taken care of the Millers' dogs last summer too. And they had really cool dogs. Both were bassett hounds. One named Brom, the other named Bowser.

The boys crossed the street and walked around to the Millers' backyard. Malcolm dug a key out from under a rock in the flowerbed, then unlocked the gate. Bowser and Brom were already there waiting. Their barks were like the last dying putts of a lawn mower.

"Hey, fellas!" Malcolm said, rubbing their necks. "Hungry?"

Brom padded over and nudged Dandy. Dandy reached down to pet him. "Wow, he's so . . . saggy."

Brom bellowed cheerfully, then rolled over for a belly rub.

"Look. He's just like you," Malcolm said with a grin.

Malcolm found the dog food sealed in a plastic tub on the back porch. Both dogs rushed him— as much as a bassett hound can rush. He scooped out a huge bowlful for each. Dandy petted Bowser as he ate.

Next Malcolm turned on the hose and cleaned out their water trough. He filled it up again and turned to Dandy. "Now the fun part."

"We play ball with them?" Dandy asked.

"Not yet." Malcolm grabbed a shovel and a bucket. "First, poop patrol."

"What?" Dandy rubbed his own belly the same way he'd rubbed Brom's earlier.

"Poop patrol," Malcolm repeated. "We can't leave it scattered all over the yard."

"Sure, we can," Dandy argued.

Malcolm gave him a look. "Come on. I've nearly stepped in it twice already." Malcolm handed Dandy the bucket. He kept the shovel. "I'll scoop."

Every time Malcolm dumped his find into the bucket, Dandy said, "Bleck!"

Once the last poop was scooped, Dandy picked up the ball. "Now do we play?"

"Go ahead," Malcolm told him. "I need to make sure their doghouse is clean."

The Millers' doghouse looked more like a playhouse than a place for dogs to sleep. Malcolm ducked in to straighten their doggie beds, but quickly jumped back. A small white dog cowered in the corner, shivering.

"Hey, little fellow," Malcolm said softly. "Where did you come from?" He hadn't realized that the Millers had gotten a new dog. He still only saw two beds. And the only bowls said *Brom* and *Bowser*.

Hmmm . . . Maybe the Millers got this dog right before they left.

"It's okay," Malcolm assured the little dog. "I'm not going to hurt you." But when he reached closer, it whimpered and thumped his tail. "All right, all right."

Malcolm backed out and grabbed more dog food. "The Millers have a new dog," he told Dandy.

Dandy stopped in mid-pitch, holding the slobbery ball he'd been tossing to the bassett hounds. "Where?"

"It's hiding in the doghouse."

Malcolm peeked in again. The dog stayed curled in the corner. "Here you go," he said, putting a small pile of food on the floor.

Malcolm waited. The dog just sat, shaking. He was afraid if he touched it the dog might snap. Better to leave it alone.

He went over to Dandy, who was wrestling the ball away from Brom. "Are they exhausted yet?" Malcolm asked.

"I don't think so." Dandy was panting harder than the dogs.

Malcolm snatched the ball from Brom's teeth, then jogged to the other side of the yard for a good throwing distance. That's when something in the kitchen window caught his eye. Just a glimpse, but it was real.

"Did you see that?" he asked Dandy.

"What?"

Malcolm crept over and peeked in. No lights were on. The house was covered in afternoon shadows. But Malcolm saw a man near the refrigerator.

Someone was inside the Millers' house!

CHAPTER FIVE

9-1-1!

Malcolm ducked. Was he imagining things?

"Dandy," he whispered. He motioned for Dandy to come over.

"What'ya hiding from?" Dandy asked in a voice loud enough to scare off birds. Brom and Bowser were jumping at him, trying to get the ball.

"Shhhh!" Malcolm put a finger to his lips.

Dandy's face went blank for a moment. Then he tiptoed over. He squatted by Malcolm under the window. Bowser and Brom followed.

"Someone's inside the Millers' house." Malcolm tried to remain calm, but his heart was thumping against his chest at record speed.

Dandy paused a moment, taking it all in. Then he asked, "Is it a man or a woman?"

"A man."
"Short or tall?"
"Tall . . . I think."
"Thin or fat?"
"Thin," Malcolm said.
"Blond hair or brown?"

"I don't know," Malcolm whispered.

"Did he have a huge, hairy mole by his nose?"

"What? I don't know, I don't think so. What difference does it make?"

Dandy leaned in. "Because if he's tall, thin, and blonde with a hairy mole, it could be Darren Von Datton, the famous diamond smuggler."

Malcolm just stared. "Do you really think the Millers have valuable diamonds hidden in their house?"

"You never know."

"I know," Malcolm said. "They don't, otherwise they would hire someone to watch their dogs instead of having the neighbor kid do it!"

Dandy rolled the ball away so Bowser and Brom would stop jumping at him. "So what now?"

"I have to be sure," Malcolm said. Inch by inch, he slowly raised himself up. He took a deep breath. Then Malcolm dared another peek. The man was still there, hovering by the fridge. Malcolm dropped back down by Dandy. "He's still there."

"Maybe it's Mr. Miller," Dandy suggested. "He could've come home early."

"But the dogs hadn't been fed. Mr. Miller would have fed them. Besides, it doesn't look like Mr. Miller."

"Maybe it's a relative. You know, an uncle or something?"

Malcolm shook his head. "The house is dark inside. Someone staying here would turn on a lamp or something."

Bowser and Brom were back, nudging Dandy. The rubber ball, full of teeth marks, was oozing slobbery goo. Dandy took it and pitched it to the back of the yard.

"So what now?" he asked again.

Malcolm mentally calculated the best approach. "Run!"

Malcolm and Dandy sped around the house to the gate. They nearly knocked it down pushing through. Malcolm closed it to keep the dogs in, but didn't bother with the lock.

Malcolm raced down the street like someone was chasing him. Dandy galloped beside him, keeping tempo with Malcolm's steps.

They nearly tripped over Cocoa in the front yard. She was stretched out in a chaise lounge, sunbathing.

"Watch it, slimeballs!" she yelled as she straightened her leopard print sunglasses with the butterscotch-yellow rhinestones.

They burst through the door, only to be met by Grandma Eunice. She was blocking their way with her wheelchair.

"Grandma, I need to get to the phone!"

"Have you seen him?" she asked, wearing a serious scowl.

"Seen who?"

"Bertram, that's who."

Malcolm fidgeted. "Grandma, no one's around right now. You don't have to pretend."

She looked Malcolm straight in the eye. He could see her eyes were bright and clear. "I'm not pretending. I know he's around. I don't need that detector of yours to feel him. Have you seen him?"

Malcolm sighed. He knew he never should have filled in Grandma Eunice on his experience at the McBleaky House. Now she thought she could hunt ghosts, too. "No, I haven't. He's not here."

"Oh, he's here all right," she said. "I can sense him." She twirled her wheelchair around in a circle. "And I want my jellybeans!"

Malcolm and Dandy whipped around her and headed for the kitchen phone.

"9-1-1, what's your emergency?"

In the calmest voice possible, Malcolm said, "I'd like to report a break-in."

CHAPTER SIX

I'M GONNA GET YOU

Malcolm and Dandy sprinted out the door. They hurdled over Cocoa and hurried off. Minutes later, they plopped down on the lawn across the street from the Millers' house.

Then they waited. And waited . . . and waited . . . and waited. It was the second time that day that Malcolm had to wait on a government worker!

"How long has it been?" Dandy asked.

"Nearly ten minutes. They should be here soon."

Dandy ran his fingers through the clumps of clover where he sat. "Maybe they got lost."

"The police don't get lost," Malcolm informed him. "They have fancy GPS systems in their cars to guide them."

"Then maybe they're all busy with a bank robbery somewhere."

"Doubtful," Malcolm said.

"Or," Dandy continued, "maybe they thought we were just a couple of kids playing a prank, and they're not coming at all."

Dandy had a point. Malcolm hadn't thought of that. But the emergency dispatcher said he'd call it in. He hadn't acted like it was a prank.

Just when Malcolm was getting worried, he saw the police cruiser turning the corner. The car rolled into the Millers' driveway, and Malcolm met the police officers who got out of the car.

"You the one who called in a break-in?" a squat, bald cop who resembled a bowling ball asked him.

"Yes, sir. The family is out of town," Malcolm told him.

The other cop leaned on the driver's side door. He was a lot younger and thinner, and his uniform looked like it was swallowing him whole.

"What are you boys doing poking around here if the family's gone?" the thin cop asked.

"I'm dogsitting for them while they're away," Malcolm quickly filled in the officers.

Dandy stood by him, twirling a clover between his fingers. His mouth was hanging open, and Malcolm knew he was amazed that he was meeting real cops.

"Okay," the bowling ball cop said. "You boys wait back over there." He pointed across the street, where they had been waiting. "We'll check it out."

Malcolm didn't hesitate. He and Dandy hurried across the street. They stood, staring as the two policemen knocked on the front door.

When no one answered, the police peeked into windows. Malcolm and Dandy watched as they disappeared into the backyard. Brom and Bowser let out a few barks, but quickly stopped.

"This feels really dangerous," Dandy said, still twirling the clover.

"Yeah," Malcolm whispered. The entire street felt hushed and quiet except for the occasional call being reported on the police car's radio. "We have a stalled car reported on Hansen Road."

Moments later the two cops emerged. The bowling ball cop looked toward them and shrugged. "Nothing in there."

Malcolm ran over. "But I saw him!"

"Maybe it was your imagination," the

driver said. "You know, a trick of the light or something."

"Someone was in the house!" Malcolm argued. "I can show you where."

Both cops sighed as they followed Malcolm to the backyard. Dandy held the dogs while Malcolm led the cops to the kitchen window.

"He was in here," Malcolm told them.

The cops framed their faces with their hands and peered in.

"I don't see anything," the skinny cop said.

"Me neither," the bowling ball cop agreed.

Malcolm peeked in, too. Right there, next to the refrigerator, stood the same man he'd seen before.

"He's right there!" Malcolm shouted, trying to point through the glass.

The cops looked in again. When they didn't see anything, they glared at Malcolm.

"Are you playing games with us, kid?" the bowling ball cop sneered. "'Cause if you are, we might need to have a talk with your parents."

"But I see him! I swear I'm not making this up. I would never waste your time," Malcolm pleaded.

The skinny cop looked around and asked, "What is that annoying beeping?"

Malcolm looked down at the waistband of his jeans. His specter detector was suddenly going berserk.

The driver snorted. "Toys. Let's go, Jake," he said to the bowling ball cop. They trudged away.

Malcolm looked at Dandy. Dandy looked at Malcolm. They both looked down at the ghost detector. Then Malcolm dared another peek in through the kitchen window.

The figure had moved closer to the window now. Malcolm could make out every detail of his transparent face.

The man grinned at Malcolm and mouthed, "I'm gonna get you."

CHAPTER SEVEN

BREAKING IN

"**G**uess we don't have to go on a ghost hunt now, huh?" Dandy said, squirming around. Brom and Bowser were back, looking up at him with begging eyes.

"Yeah, but we only have the ghost detector with. I forgot to bring the ghost zapper," Malcolm complained.

"So now what?" Dandy asked, still wiggly.

"We come back after dinner," Malcolm said. "We can zap that ugly mullet then."

"We're not going in now?" Dandy asked with a relieved sigh.

"No," Malcolm answered. "We have to prepare."

"Good," Dandy said, wriggling like crazy. "'Cause I have to use the bathroom."

• • •

That evening Malcolm ripped into his fried chicken and mashed potatoes. He was eager to get a move on since this was his big chance to test the ghost zapper.

He was also eager to get away from the table. Cocoa had stayed outside too long and now had big white circles around her eyes where her sunglasses had been. She looked like a giant strawberry with a fungus.

"I'd rather have jellybeans!" Grandma Eunice complained through the entire meal. Malcolm shoveled his food down quickly to get away as fast as possible. The last thing he needed was for his mom to say he had to stay home with his grandma tonight.

He couldn't help but worry though. The ghost told him, "I'm gonna get you." Malcolm didn't take kindly to threats. Not even ghost threats. But he definitely had to proceed with caution.

The late afternoon sun hung low in the west. One thin cloud crossed it so it looked like a basketball sailing though the net. It was still a couple of hours 'til dark.

Malcolm waited for Dandy in the Millers'

front yard. He had already turned the ghost detector to On so it'd be warmed up and ready.

Dandy approached commando style, ducking behind shrubs and the gate. He was wearing earmuffs and tinted safety goggles. He looked like a scientist CIA operative in the Arctic.

"What's all that for?" Malcolm asked.

"Huh?" Dandy said.

Malcolm removed the earmuffs. "What's with the extra gear?"

"The detector hypnotized me last time. I didn't want to take any chances."

Dandy made a good point. "I think it might be okay as long as you don't look at the blinking light too long," Malcolm explained.

"Oh," Dandy said, disappointed. "Can I keep the goggles on? They make everything look like I'm underwater." He did a mock breaststroke.

"Sure," Malcolm said. They headed around back.

Dandy stopped to pet the dogs. "Hey, Bowser. Hey, Brom."

Brom answered with a burpy-sounding bark.

"Shhhh!" Malcolm warned. "We want the element of surprise."

Dandy grinned. "I love surprises."

"Not a surprise for us, Dandy. We want to surprise the ghost . . . catch him off guard."

Dandy nodded, putting a finger to his lips. Then, the boys tiptoed toward the window.

Malcolm heard a yipping noise and looked toward the doghouse. There stood the small white dog. He was shaking.

Malcolm decided to check on the pooch once the Millers' ghost had been zapped. The poor thing looked frightened.

Malcolm peered into the window. Nothing was there. He scanned the entire kitchen.

"You see anything?" Dandy whispered.

"Not yet."

Malcolm's gaze moved to the open area that went from the kitchen to the living room. There, the ghost was lounging on the sofa, staring at the blank TV.

"Wait! I see him. Looks like he's watching ghost TV."

"Neat!" Dandy said. "I wonder what they show on that channel . . ."

Malcolm motioned Dandy closer. "We have to find a way in."

They tried the window. Locked.

They tried the back door. Locked.

"We could slide down the chimney," Dandy suggested.

"That's too dangerous."

Dandy shrugged. "Maybe for you. But I'm wearing safety goggles, remember?"

"I've got a better idea," Malcolm told him. He stepped up onto the plastic container of dog food and ran his fingers along the top of the back door.

"Not there," he said. He jumped down and lifted the doormat. Nothing. Then he shoved the large dog food container aside. There it was— a shiny brass key.

Malcolm held it up in triumph. "See? This is better than sliding down the chimney."

Dandy shrugged. Malcolm could tell that Dandy was a tad disappointed. He knew Dandy had been ready to see how it felt to be Santa Claus.

As quietly as humanly possible, Malcolm slipped the key in and unlocked the door.

CHAPTER EIGHT

COME OUT, COME OUT, WHEREVER YOU ARE

C*lick!* Malcolm opened the door in slow-motion, careful of what might jump out. He looked left . . . then right. All clear.

He gently placed a foot inside. That's when Bowser and Brom decided to serenade them with some lonesome howls. It all felt too eerie to Malcolm.

Dandy crept in behind Malcolm and was about to shut the door. "Wait," Malcolm whispered. "Let's leave it open . . . just in case."

"In case of what?" Dandy whispered back, his goggles crooked on his face.

Malcolm wanted to say, "In case we have to make a run for it." But he didn't want to sound like a coward. "I think it's just safer that way," he said instead.

Dandy cocked his head to the side. "But what if the ghost gets out?"

"Then it probably won't haunt the Millers' house anymore and our job will be done."

Dandy looked thoughtful. "But I thought we're here to zap it, not chase it away." He made a vibrating motion like he was being zapped.

"We are," Malcolm argued. "But let's keep our options open, okay?"

"Okay," Dandy agreed. "We'll keep the door open . . . just like our options."

They tiptoed across the kitchen. Malcolm had his ghost detector at the ready. The amber light bleeped one pulse per second, meaning there was no ghost activity at the moment.

"Here's the plan," he whispered. "Once the ghost shows himself, I'll whip out the zapper and spray. Easy, right?"

"Shouldn't you keep it aimed?" Dandy wondered.

"I can draw it out fast," Malcolm said. He flipped his arm quickly to show Dandy his speed.

"But I thought you had to shake it first," Dandy reminded him.

"I'll shake it as I pull it out."

"You want me to hold it?" Dandy asked, adjusting his goggles.

"No! What if he recognizes what it is? It'll scare him off and we won't have a chance to zap him."

Dandy scrunched his face, confused. "Then he'll run out the kitchen door and our job will be done, right?"

"Just stay with me," Malcolm said, once again moving across the kitchen floor. Butterflies danced in his belly.

Bleep . . . bleep . . . bleep . . . bleep . . .

Malcolm moved cautiously, aiming the detector. He pointed it everywhere. At the oven. The refrigerator. The microwave.

"You think the ghost could be hiding in there?" Dandy asked.

Malcolm nodded. "Ghosts can fold themselves into anything."

"Really? 'Cause I saw a girl once at a magic show who could fold herself up and crawl into a cereal box."

"That was an illusion, Dandy. She didn't really fit into the cereal box."

"She could have," he said. "There wasn't any cereal in it."

Malcolm ignored him and kept his pace. The detector continued bleeping. He moved on, slinking through the kitchen.

He peered into the living room. The sun had dropped farther in the sky, and Malcolm had to squint to see into the darkened room. No ghost on the couch. The clock on the mantel kept time with the detector.

Malcolm aimed the specter detector at everything, including the portrait of the Millers. The family of four grinned "cheese!" out of the frame at him.

"Maybe we should turn on a light," Dandy said.

Malcolm shook his head. "It's not that dark."

"I can barely see a thing."

He heard Dandy stumble and saw him feeling around for objects in front of him. "Take off those goggles," Malcolm whispered.

"Oh, yeah." Dandy reluctantly pulled them down where they dangled around his neck.

Bleep, bleep, bleep, bleep, bleep, bleep!

The light on the ghost detector began to blink faster.

Suddenly, the TV clicked on. Malcolm jumped. Then he saw the remote lying on the coffee table, untouched. Yikes!

"Gee, I wonder what's on the ghost channel," Dandy said.

Only static and snow. Just as Malcolm reached for the remote, the picture cleared. A creepy phantom face looked out at them and grinned. "I'm gonna get you!"

CHAPTER NINE
GHOST HUNT

Malcolm clicked the off button on the TV several times. Dandy scrambled to put his goggles back on.

"Dude, what are you doing?" Malcolm yelled to him.

"I liked it better when I couldn't see!" Dandy said.

"Dandy!"

The phantom winked at Malcolm, and then the screen faded to black. Malcolm shivered so hard he could barely hold the ghost detector steady.

Bleep . . . bleep . . . bleep . . . bleep . . .

"Why didn't you zap it?" Dandy asked.

"Because it wasn't really here. It was on TV. We've never used the ghost zapper, so we don't know what it will do. Who knows what would've happened if I'd zapped the screen."

"Yeah, and it is a flat-screen. That would've been expensive to replace," Dandy reasoned. "What'd we do now?"

Malcolm wondered that too. He glanced back at the TV. It now looked like a giant black hole, ready to swallow him up. He backed away quickly.

"Maybe we should look around some more."

"O-Okay," Dandy said, trying to sound brave.

Bleep . . . bleep . . . bleep . . . bleep . . .

The ghost detector was still at one bleep per second. Malcolm felt safe for the moment. "This way," he said.

He slowly inched his way to the hall, leading to the Millers' bedrooms. He'd barely taken two steps into it when he heard a loud crash! Malcolm flipped on the light and turned. Dandy lay sprawled out on the floor, face down. "Dandy!"

"Sorry," Dandy said, his voice muffled by the carpet. "I fell over the coffee table."

"Take off those goggles!"

Dandy did what Malcolm said, even though

he felt safer with the goggles on. He caught up
to Malcolm in the hallway.

Both boys stepped lightly. Malcolm held the
detector with his left hand. He kept his right
hand clutched around the zapper. He wasn't
taking chances. This nasty ghost could jump out
at any moment, and Malcolm wanted to be able
to whip out the zapper fast.

The boys crept up to the first bedroom.
Malcolm peeked around the doorjamb. It was
Katie Miller's room. She was the Millers' oldest
daughter who went to high school. The walls
were plastered with movie posters and silly
street signs.

Bleep, bleep, bleep, bleep, bleep, bleep!

Dandy tapped Malcolm on the shoulder.
"Does that guy look familiar to you?" He
pointed to a poster of the old movie, *Gone with
the Wind*. It showed the lead actor, Clark Gable,
dipping the lead actress, Vivien Leigh. They were
just about to kiss.

Malcolm took a step closer. *Gone with the
Wind* was one of Grandma Eunice's favorite
movies. She made Malcolm watch it with her
nearly every time he had to "watch" her for his

parents. Malcolm could tell right away that this was not Clark Gable or any other character from the movie.

As though coming to life, the man's head turned and grinned at them. "I'm gonna get you!"

Malcolm pulled out the zapper and shook it

hard. But as he aimed it, the face on the poster faded back to the original actor.

"Rats!" Malcolm yelled.

"I-I d-don't th-th-think we're going to g-get this one," Dandy said. His voice echoed like a stadium announcer's.

"I'm not giving up so easy," Malcolm announced.

This ghost was playing games with them. Like ghost hide-and-seek. There had to be a way to get him. Malcolm headed back into the hall.

Bleep . . . bleep . . . bleep . . . bleep . . .

"Come on," he told Dandy.

They did the usual tiptoe toward the next room.

"Who do you think it is?" Dandy asked.

"Who do I think who is?" Malcolm replied.

"The ghost. Who do you think he is and why do you think he's haunting the Millers' house?"

"I don't know," Malcolm said. "But he shouldn't be here."

"Maybe he should," Dandy argued. "Maybe he's guarding the house while the Millers are away."

"A guard ghost? I don't think so. He's not wearing a guard uniform or anything."

"Good point," Dandy said.

The next door led to the parents' bedroom. Malcolm flicked on the light and scanned the room. It was decorated with a blue striped bedspread, red striped curtains, and green striped wallpaper. The whole room looked like it was surrounded by bars.

Bleep, bleep, bleep, bleep, bleep, bleep!

Dandy headed toward a desk in the corner. "Look. They left their computer on. Let's Google something."

Malcolm pulled Dandy back fast. One of the fish bobbing along the screensaver turned and swam toward them.

"I'm gonna get you!" it gurgled. One of the bubbles floated off the screen and exploded near Dandy's face. He fell back on his bottom. The computer clicked off on its own.

"That's it!" Malcolm yelled. "I'm going to find you!" He pulled Dandy to his feet, and they stomped out of the room.

The next door he came to was shut. It was the bathroom. Malcolm only knew this because he could hear water running.

"Somebody's taking a shower," Dandy said.

Malcolm creaked the door open.

"I don't think we should go in," Dandy told him. "What if he's on the toilet?"

Malcolm ignored Dandy and opened the door. He motioned Dandy to follow him.

The shower curtain was drawn, and the room was covered in a hazy mist. "Look!" Dandy said, pointing to the mirror. Scrawled in the fogged up mirror were the words, *I'm gonna get you!*

Malcolm whipped around and pulled back the shower curtain. Nothing.

"One more room left to check," Malcolm said. But they never got the chance. As soon as the boys turned into hall, the ghost jumped down behind them and yelled, "Got you!"

CHAPTER TEN
GOT YOU!

Bleeeeeeeeeeeeeeeeeeeeeeeeeeeeeep!

Dandy screamed like a banshee while Malcolm shook the zapper. But before he pressed the trigger, the ghost huffed a horrendous breath at them. It knocked them down with hurricane force winds and sent the zapper flying out of Malcolm's hand.

"Ew!" Dandy said, waving his hand in front of his nose. "That smells like onions and feet!"

Malcolm couldn't argue. That ghost did have stinky breath. But he was more concerned with getting the zapper so he could finish this ghost off.

The ghost dived at them. The boys scrambled and ran. Malcolm saw the zapper had landed near the fireplace. He hurried toward it, but

the ghost popped down, blocking his way.
He reached his long bogeyman arms toward
Malcolm.

"Do something!" Malcolm yelled.

Dandy grabbed his goggles by the strap and
swung them at the ghost. "Take that!"

The ghost grabbed the goggles and pulled.
Dandy pulled too. The strap stretched and
stretched.

"Let go!" Malcolm cried.

Too late. The ghost let go first. The goggles
snapped back, hitting Dandy in the head and
knocking him flat . . . again.

"Ouch," he said groggily.

Malcolm needed to get that zapper! Or
maybe he just needed to get away. The ghost
tilted his head, looking at him this way and
that. When he grinned again, he showed a full
set of razor-like teeth. He started toward them.

Malcolm tried to get Dandy to his feet. The
ghost moved closer . . . and closer . . . and . . .
stopped.

The ghost's sneer turned to surprise.
Malcolm heard snarling and looked down. The
little white dog had come in through the open

kitchen door and was biting the ghost's leg. He was even dragging him backward.

The ghost tried shaking him off. He jumped and kicked and twisted his leg. The fierce little dog held on tight. The distraction was exactly what Malcolm needed. He grabbed the ghost zapper and shook.

When the ghost turned back it was Malcolm's turn to grin and yell, "I'm gonna get you!"

The little dog let go as Malcolm pulled the trigger. The zapper sprayed the specter with a thick spatter of purple ooze. The ooze looked a lot like whipped cream, but it smelled like cotton candy.

The ghost stood frozen in goo. Then he and the goo slowly melted into nothing more than a large wet stain on the carpet.

The little dog sniffed it. *Yip! Yip!*

"Yes!" Malcolm cheered.

Dandy sat up, rubbing his forehead. "Is it over?"

"Yeah," Malcolm answered. "Thanks to this little fellow—" But when he turned back, the little dog had already run off.

Dandy looked at the large wet spot on the carpet. "Did the dog do that?"

Malcolm smiled. "Not exactly. Come on, let's go." He pointed to the big purple lump now forming just above Dandy's eyes. "You need to put some ice on that."

Malcolm helped his friend up and they hurried out. Then, he locked the back door and put the key back in its place under the plastic container. Brom and Bowser had joined them on the porch. Bowser held the rubber ball in his jowls.

"Not now," Malcolm said. He looked out at the doghouse. Was the brave little white dog curled up in the corner? He didn't have time to check. It was dark now, and he needed to get home.

When they reached the front yard, Malcolm turned to Dandy. "Thanks," he said.

Dandy looked puzzled. "For what?"

"For helping me out. I would've been too scared to do this alone."

"Yeah, me too. It's too bad we'll never know who that ghost was," Dandy said.

They left the Millers' house, ghost-free, and headed home.

CHAPTER ELEVEN

SPOOKY

Malcolm walked Dandy to his house and made sure he put an ice pack on his forehead. It was late by the time he got home.

He was met with a surprise as he reached his front porch.

Bleep, bleep, bleep, bleep, bleep, bleep!

The specter detector was going off like crazy. Malcolm had forgotten to turn it off. As he reached to get it out of his pocket, he had a second surprise.

Yip! Yip! Yip!

The little dog from the Millers' house sat on his porch, excitedly wagging his tail.

"Hey, fella," Malcolm said, bending down. "How'd you find my house?"

The dog answered with *Yip!*

The dog didn't have a collar like Bowser and Brom. And Malcolm hadn't seen an extra bowl or bed back at the Millers'. There was really no sign that the dog belonged to them.

The mutt sat, looking up at Malcolm with large pleading eyes. Malcolm had never owned a dog, thanks to Cocoa and her sneezing fits. But maybe he could sneak this one in and keep it in his lab. At least for a while.

"Okay, you win," Malcolm said. He reached down to pick up the dog. To his amazement, his hand passed right through it.

Malcolm jumped back. "Whoa! That's spooky."

Yip! Yip! The ghostly dog excitedly wagged his tail.

"Spooky," Malcolm repeated. "Come on, Spooky. Come on, boy." He opened his front door, and his new dog, Spooky, ran in.

The house was dark and quiet. Exhausted, Malcolm decided to go straight to bed. There'd been way too much excitement tonight.

As they trudged through the kitchen, Spooky began to bark and the ghost detector started bleeping up a storm. Malcolm looked around.

To his amazement, a transparent man stood in the doorway!

Startled, Malcolm jumped. The man was wearing a powder-blue '70s leisure suit and was smiling at him. Malcolm thought about grabbing

his ghost zapper, but this apparition didn't appear menacing at all. In fact, he looked kind and proud. Malcolm then saw a bit of family resemblance.

"Grandpa Bertram, is that you?"

Grandpa Bertram nodded. Without a word, he pointed to the kitchen table, then disappeared.

Malcolm looked down to see a small bag filled with jellybeans. He picked them up, careful not to mess up the lovely blue ribbon attached. He quietly crept to Grandma Eunice's room and placed them on her night table.

Then Malcolm happily went off to bed. When he turned off the specter detector, Spooky disappeared. He quickly turned it back on and could see his new pooch. He smiled, knowing for certain that Cocoa wouldn't be having sneezing fits with this pet!

Malcolm said good night to Spooky, shut off his ghost detector, and fell into a dead sleep.

BOOK 3
TELL NO ONE!

CHAPTER ONE

THE DAY BEFORE

Malcolm and his best friend, Dandy, sat quietly in Malcolm's basement lab. It was one of those late afternoons, right before dinner, when you wish there were more hours left to hang out. Malcolm was perched on an old desk, while Dandy slumped lazily in a beanbag chair.

"I can't believe it went by so fast," Malcolm complained. He flipped on his Ecto-Handheld-Automatic-Heat-Sensitive- Laser-Enhanced Specter Detector. It was the gadget he used for hunting ghosts.

With the specter detector on, he could play with his new dog, Spooky. Spooky was a phantom canine that had recently followed Malcolm home. He eagerly wagged his tail at Malcolm.

"I can't believe summer is already over," Malcolm said, as he put his chin in his hand. "It seems like we just started ghost hunting yesterday."

"Summer always goes fast," Dandy reminded him.

"Yeah, but this one went too fast." His hangdog expression practically touched the floor.

"Look at the bright side," Dandy said. "We're fifth graders this year."

That was true. Malcolm did like the idea of being in the highest grade at Waxberry Elementary.

Dandy chewed a fingernail. "I bet fifth grade will be a lot harder than fourth."

"Yeah," Malcolm agreed.

"But we'll get to ride in the very back of the bus," Dandy continued.

"That's the bumpiest part!" Malcolm said.

Dandy suddenly sat forward. "Oh no, I just remembered—fifth graders have the last lunch of the day!"

Malcolm shook his head. "Let's hope there's enough food left."

Dandy looked like he'd just dropped his
last piece of gum on the floor. The only lively
creature in the basement was Malcolm's ghostly
pet. *Yip! Yip!* Spooky hopped and bounced,
jumping at Malcolm to play.

Malcolm scooted off the desk, onto the floor. Spooky tried to grab Malcolm's shirt for tug-of-war, but his teeth went right through the shirt.

Once Spooky learned he couldn't hang on, he decided a game of run-through-Malcolm would be more fun. He dashed in and out, one side then the other.

"Stop, Spooky. That tickles! Sit!"

Spooky sat eagerly, tail wagging.

Malcolm looked at Dandy and sighed. "You know the worst part of going back to school?"

Dandy slid another finger in his mouth and chewed on that nail. "There's something worse than 12:45 lunch?"

"We can only ghost hunt on weekends."

Malcolm and Dandy had already had two exciting ghost adventures this summer. First, they'd gone into the Freaky McBleaky house and been chased out by the ghost Herbert McBleaky. Malcolm still cringed at the thought of the major wedgie the jokester had given him.

Then, Malcolm waited weeks for his Ecto-Handheld-Automatic-Heat-Sensitive- Laser-Enhanced Ghost Zapper to arrive. When it finally did, he went ghost hunting again. He zapped a ghost at the Millers' house—and met his late great-grandfather and Spooky!

"And we were just getting started," Dandy said.

Malcolm fidgeted with his specter detector, flipping it off and on. Spooky flicked off and on, too. He faded then returned, over and over, as the specter detector detected him.

"We won't let it end. Ghost hunting is what we do," Malcolm said, trying to sound encouraging. "We'll devote every weekend to searching out ghosts."

"Right," Dandy agreed.

"Nothing will stand in our way."

Dandy straightened, chin high. "Yep. Nothing."

Malcolm was starting to cheer up. "On weekends, ghost hunting comes first!"

"Right," Dandy said. "Ghost hunting comes first. Right after I do my homework . . . mow the lawn . . . clean my room . . . and bathe the dog." He counted out each item on his fingers.

Malcolm's cheerful mood quickly drooped. "We'll find time."

It was then that the basement door burst

open. A voice much like a bullhorn blared, "Mom says it's time for dinner, snothead!"

Malcolm's sister, Cocoa, stood at the top of the stairs. She wore Irish green eye shadow and clown red lip gloss. Malcolm thought she looked like a traffic light.

Spooky was scared by Cocoa's demanding presence. He dashed straight through Malcolm and hid behind him.

"Tell Mom I'll be there in a minute," Malcolm said.

Cocoa glared, hands on hips. "I'm not your messenger. Now come eat. And tell your goofy friend he has to go home." Her lips curled into a devilish grin. "It's a school night."

He couldn't think of anything clever to say, so Malcolm simply stuck out his tongue.

"Nerd!" Cocoa yelled, stomping away.

Malcolm turned to Dandy. "There is one good thing about going back to school tomorrow."

"What's that?" Dandy wondered.

"Seven full hours away from her!"

CHAPTER TWO
UP AND AT 'EM

Eeg . . . eeg . . . eeg . . .

The only sound worse than Cocoa's annoying screech was that of the alarm clock. The sound made Malcolm want to shed his skin. He slapped the off button and tumbled out of bed.

His plan to visit the bathroom failed when he discovered his sister had made camp in there.

"You're not the only person in this house, you know!" Malcolm loudly reminded her.

"It's the first day of school!" she called back through the closed door. "I have to look perfect!"

"If that's what you're waiting for, you'll be in there for eternity," Malcolm muttered as he walked away.

He tried his parents' bathroom, but Grandma Eunice occupied it. She'd obviously finished her morning prunes.

Malcolm gave up and headed to the kitchen for breakfast. He dropped two pieces of bread into the toaster. While he waited, he remembered the time he'd tried converting that very toaster into an alien heat ray.

When the toast was ready, he poured a glass of orange juice. His mom had already put the peanut butter and bananas on the table.

Malcolm plopped into his chair. It scraped as he scooted closer. His parents were still eating, and they glanced up at all the noise he was making.

"I can't believe my babies are growing up so fast," Malcolm's mom said. Her voice was as sweet as the apple-mint jelly she smeared on her muffin.

His dad just grunted. Malcolm guessed he hadn't had a chance at the bathroom either.

"And it's already the first day of school," Mom continued.

"Please, don't remind me," Malcolm said, sipping some juice.

Mom sniffed the air. "It even smells like the first day. I can smell the newly sharpened pencils, chalk dust, and Big Chief tablets."

"What are Big Chief tablets?"

"That's what we used when your dad and I were little. Right, dear?" she said to Dad.

Dad grunted again. He never looked up from staring at his coffee.

The bathroom door flew open, rattling the entire house. "MOM!" Cocoa shrieked.

She stood in the doorway, wearing a violet shirt, purple skirt, plum-colored hoop earrings, and lavender tie-dyed sneakers. The indigo tint of her nail polish, eye shadow, and lip gloss looked like something from the "undead" cosmetic line.

Cocoa reminded Malcolm of an enormous grape. If she stood there for about 40 years, she could pass for a California raisin.

"Mom!" she whined this time. "Look!" She held out her shirt and pointed near the hem.

"What is it, sweetie?" Mom asked.

"Look!" Cocoa said again.

Mom squinted. "Look at what?"

Cocoa moved closer. "This!"

Mom squinted more. "I don't see anything."

"Of course not! The rhinestone heart fell off!" Cocoa drooped and sobbed like she just flunked history or something. Tears gushed down her cheeks. Malcolm didn't see what the big deal was, but that was a girl for you.

"No one will notice," Mom assured her soothingly.

"That's what I'm afraid of!" Cocoa stomped her foot. "No one will notice this awesome outfit."

Malcolm didn't know about awesome. But now that Cocoa was no longer blocking the doorway, he saw his chance at the bathroom. Before he could move a muscle, Cocoa whipped around.

"Now I have to rethink the whole thing. I must look perfect for the first day!" she yelled. She clomped back to the bathroom, slamming the door.

"Hey!" Malcolm called. "Your clothes are in your bedroom!"

"But crying smeared my makeup, dufus. I have to redo it!"

For once Malcolm looked forward to his first day of school—just so he could use the boys' room!

CHAPTER THREE

SLOW RIDE

The back of the school bus was indeed the bumpiest part. Malcolm wondered if the bus driver, Mr. Mullins, actually aimed for every pothole in the road. The boys were trapped in the far corner amid a crowd of chattering students.

Dandy yawned. "It's bumpy and hot back here. It's not as great as I thought it would be."

"No kidding," Malcolm said. He tried pulling down a window, but no amount of tugging would free it.

Malcolm gave up and slumped down in his seat. But then he remembered something important. He reached into his backpack and pulled out his digital camera.

"What's that for?" Dandy asked. Sweat beads had formed on his nose like teeny raindrops.

"Pictures," Malcolm answered. "This year we're part of the yearbook staff, remember?"

Malcolm hadn't really wanted to be on the yearbook staff, but he was talked into it because they needed a photographer.

At first he'd resisted, but then he imagined all the cool things he could do with the photos. There was no limit to the fancy photo effects he could dream up.

He was already planning to swap the principal's head with the school mascot, a hornet. And he may even add bubbles to the noses of the student council. Malcolm was set to make this year's Waxberry Elementary yearbook the best ever.

Dandy scratched his nose, smearing the dirty sweat. "I don't know how to put together a yearbook."

"It's not hard. Remember when we were in kindergarten, and we made those placemats for Thanksgiving?" Malcolm asked.

Dandy nodded, looking confused. His finger slipped around to the other side of his nose. "Yeah. We glued old photos to a piece of construction paper."

"Well, it's sort of the same thing," Malcolm explained, playing with the strap of the camera.

Dandy's finger slid from his nose to his lip. He kept scratching. "But I ended up with more paste on the top than on the bottom. Everyone on my placemat had a milk mustache."

Milk mustaches . . . *Got Homework?* That was a great idea for the faculty picture!

"I don't think I'm going to be very good at working on the yearbook," Dandy added.

"Don't worry, Dandy. You can be my assistant and help me take pictures."

"That's no good. I usually end up with pictures of my fingers," Dandy said.

That was true. Malcolm remembered several years ago when he had found a footprint so large it could only have belonged to Bigfoot. It was starting to rain, so right then was his only chance to show proof. He'd lain down next to the huge track to give it scale. Then he had Dandy snap the photo.

When they uploaded the photos, Dandy's big orangey thumb covered the entire footprint. Malcolm had looked like he was being slammed by a giant meteor.

"How about I do the picture taking," Malcolm suggested. "You can pose the subjects."

Dandy sat forward, resting his elbows on his knees. "I guess I could do that."

"Of course you can. You'll be great at it," Malcolm encouraged his friend.

The bus bounced and jolted its way around
a few more blocks, stopping every couple
of minutes to cram in more kids. Then the
Waxberry marquee came into view.

Welcome back to Waxberry for another great
year! Go Hornets!

Some of the kids cheered. Some groaned.
Dandy yawned. The first thing Malcolm did
after he got off the bus was snap a picture of
the marquee. He had big plans for the yearbook
photos. Nothing was going to mess that up.

CHAPTER FOUR

GRUELING GOOLSBY

Malcolm snapped a few more pictures of the morning bustle. He caught kids rushing to class and teachers smiling through clenched teeth on film.

He also caught Coss Fitzfox, last year's Kickball King, hobbling in on crutches. He snapped a picture of "Booger" McCready, chess champion, walking the halls with a pair of soccer cleats slung over his shoulder. And he captured Waxberry's rough-and-ready tomboy, Candace Dillion, wearing mascara.

"You can't make this stuff up," Malcolm told Dandy. They headed for the bulletin board in the cafeteria to check which rooms they were assigned.

"I hope we're in the same class again," Dandy said, heaving his enormous backpack. With every step he appeared to be trudging through syrup.

It didn't take long to find their names. "Look!" Dandy said. "We are in the same room."

Malcolm smiled. "Yep." Then he checked the room number. Yikes! Room 503! Mrs. Goolsby! Grueling Goolsby, the toughest teacher in the entire school.

"Oh no! We're doomed." Dandy dropped his backpack with a thud.

Malcolm couldn't agree more.

Dandy dragged his backpack behind him as they headed for that fateful room.

Mrs. Goolsby stood by the classroom door. She tapped a ruler on her palm as students ducked in. Malcolm figured she couldn't wait to shut the door and begin the torture.

Malcolm debated whether or not to take her picture. *Not a good idea*, he concluded.

When they took their seats, Dandy whispered, "I guess we won't get to ghost hunt now, huh?"

True. There probably wouldn't be another free weekend until next summer. Malcolm had heard that Mrs. Goolsby even assigned homework during the winter holidays! "Maybe it won't be so bad," he said. But secretly, he knew better.

The sweat beads had returned to Dandy's nose. His eyes were filled with panic. "Maybe we could transfer out."

Malcolm shrugged. "Doubtful."

"Maybe our parents would agree to homeschool us."

"Even more doubtful," Malcolm said as the bell rang.

"Quiet!" Mrs. Goolsby called, the door sweeping shut. "Pull out your math books and turn to Chapter One."

Among the groans Dandy said, "But we haven't even heard the announcements."

"Who said that?" Mrs. Goolsby asked, her eyes piercing each person.

Dandy slowly raised a shaky hand.

"What is your name?" she demanded.

Dandy gulped. "Daniel. Daniel Dee."

"Well, Mr. Dee," Mrs. Goolsby sneered. "I bet you can do at least one problem before the announcements. Let's see, shall we?"

Dandy gulped again, much louder. "What about attendance?"

Mrs. Goolsby slapped the ruler hard across the edge of her desk, causing an explosive noise that could've set off a panic bell. "It's my job to worry about attendance, Mr. Dee. It's your job to get those problems done. Stop wasting time!"

The kids scurried for their books and pencils. Malcolm saw Dandy staring at the blunt nub of his, and knew he was too frightened to get up and use the pencil sharpener.

They worked the math problems, only stopping to say the Pledge of Allegiance. Mrs. Goolsby strolled by each desk. She paused at Malcolm's desk. "What's this?" She held up the camera.

"I'm taking pictures for the yearbook," he answered.

"Are you taking pictures at this very moment?" she grilled.

"No," Malcolm said. Now he was doing the gulping.

"Then . . . put . . . it . . . away," she rolled out each word like she was speaking a foreign language.

Malcolm did as he was told.

As the day progressed, it didn't get much better. There were no introductory games in Mrs. Goolsby's class. No working in teams like in fourth grade. Just hour after hour of Math, English, Science, and History.

Malcolm did manage to take more pictures. But that was during lunch, recess, and Mrs. Flutterfly's art class. When the three o'clock bell rang, Malcolm was the first in line for the school bus. He couldn't wait to get home.

After a couple of cookies and lemonade, he relayed the dreadful events of the day to his mom. "Mrs. Goolsby's a velociraptor in loafers!" he said.

"Oh, Malcolm," Mom sighed. "You have such an imagination."

Malcolm knew he wasn't going to get any sympathy. So, he headed to the computer to upload the yearbook photos before he started his pile of homework.

He checked them one by one. Then, he checked them again. He looked at his camera, then back to the pictures on his computer. He zoomed in closer and checked again. Then Malcolm dashed to the phone.

"Dandy, get over here quick! Our ghost hunting days are not over!"

CHAPTER FIVE

TELL NO ONE!

"**I** don't get it," Dandy said, looking from the computer screen to the photo printouts. He twitched his nose like he was about to sneeze.

"I don't either," Malcolm said. "It's the weirdest thing that's ever happened to me."

Dandy gave him a look.

"Okay, maybe not the weirdest, but it comes pretty close."

"Who is that guy?" Dandy asked.

Malcolm had no idea. He looked at the photos again. The picture of the school marquee came out just fine. But instead of *Go Hornets!* it said *TELL NO ONE!* And next to the marquee stood an odd-looking man. Odd, for a couple reasons.

1. He wore a green khaki fishing cap and vest, both covered in various fishing hooks and lures.
2. The man was transparent. No doubt, a ghost!

Malcolm checked out the close-up he'd taken of Candace Dillion. He caught her mid-blink. But instead of eye makeup, there was writing on both her eyelids.

Left eyelid: *TELL*

Right eyelid: *NO ONE!*

And standing directly behind her was the ghostly fisherman.

Malcolm studied the photo of Booger McCready. Booger's T-shirt now sported the words, *TELL NO ONE!* The fisherman lurked nearby.

And the picture of Coss Fitzfox clearly showed *TELL NO ONE!* written across the cast on his leg. The phantom fisherman peeked over his shoulder.

Malcolm scrolled through the same photos on the computer. "The school is definitely haunted," he told Dandy.

"It could be a glitch in the camera," Dandy suggested.

"You mean like a mechanical failure?"

Daddy nodded. "Yeah. A glitch."

"I double-checked it, Dandy. Besides, a glitch would probably cause lots of blobs or something. Not this."

"Maybe it's a double-exposure."

"Of what?" Malcolm argued. "I've never taken any pictures with those words on them . . . or that guy. I've never seen him before. And digital cameras don't make double-exposures."

"Did you have your specter detector with you?" Dandy wondered.

Malcolm shook his head no. He picked up the detector and flipped it to On. He liked the sound it made warming up. Then he switched it to Detect.

Yip! Yip! Spooky appeared, as if he'd been patiently waiting to be noticed by the specter detector and Malcolm.

"Hey, Spooky! I missed you today."

The dog bounced and wagged his tail.

Dandy leaned down and pretended to pet the dog. His hand brushed completely through the pooch, but Spooky's face showed he appreciated the gesture.

Malcolm went back to studying the photo. "I just wish I knew what this meant," he said.

Dandy continued fake-petting Spooky. "We'll have to figure it out later. Can you believe all the homework Mrs. Goolsby gave us? I'm going to be up way past my bedtime."

Malcolm groaned. "No kidding. And on the first day! What teacher assigns a 1,000-word essay on the lessons we learned over summer vacation and how they relate to the writings of Roald Dahl?"

"Mrs. Goolsby!" Dandy complained. Even Spooky let out a *Yip! Yip!*

Malcolm turned off his specter detector, sending Spooky back to invisible realms. Then he and Dandy trudged up the steps of the basement lab.

"Even though we can't do it tonight, we have to find out who that guy is," Malcolm said. "We need to know why he's haunting the school."

"Well, whoever he is," Dandy said, "his instructions are clear. We can't tell anyone! And I'm not going to go against any ghost's wishes."

CHAPTER SIX
A MUDDY EXCUSE

Malcolm took his camera to school early the next day. He took pictures of the marquee, the cafeteria, and the library before heading to class.

"I've got to test it," he told Dandy. "I've got to find out why he's haunting the school. I'm going to take as many pictures as I can."

Dandy's backpack looked even heavier than yesterday. His stroll down the hall looked more like a trek up a steep mountain. "Maybe he used to be a school teacher or P.E. coach here."

"But why the fishing getup?" Malcolm reasoned. "Shouldn't he be haunting a lake house, or a fishing boat, or Angler Bob's Bait Shop instead?"

Dandy adjusted his backpack. As he did, his

knees buckled a little. "Maybe there used to be a lake here, and the school was built over it."

"Don't be silly, Dandy. Where would they've put all the water?"

"Well, our toilets have been overflowing a lot."

As they were about to step into the classroom, Mrs. Goolsby cried, "Oh, no you don't!"

Malcolm and Dandy froze.

"Look at your shoes!" she yelled at them. Her face had flushed a heated pink, and her eyes zapped them like lasers. "Caked in mud! I will not have you soiling my classroom!"

The boys just looked at each other. Neither one was sure what to do. After all, they'd never seen a teacher so upset about a little dirt.

"Remove your shoes this instant," she instructed, "and set them by the door. You will spend your recess in the boys' room cleaning them. Understood?"

They both nodded, afraid to speak.

"Now take your seats!"

They scrambled to get their sneakers off. Once they were seated, Mrs. Goolsby drilled them through a morning of nonstop lectures, lessons, and practice sheets. Malcolm wondered if it was possible for a person's brain to overload and short-circuit.

. . .

"Getting mud on our shoes turned out to be lucky," Malcolm told Dandy as the other kids lined up for recess.

Dandy scrunched his eyebrows. "Why was that lucky? She's scarier than the ghost fisherman!"

Malcolm grinned. "It was lucky because the computer lab is empty this time of day."

"We can't clean our shoes in the computer lab!" Dandy argued. "We'll get detention."

"We're not going to clean our shoes, silly," Malcolm said impatiently.

Panic flashed across Dandy's face. "If we don't clean our shoes, we'll get detention for sure!"

"We'll clean our shoes later. Follow me, we've got ghost hunting to do."

Dandy followed, trudging like he still had his backpack on. He held his dirty sneakers by the laces, letting them sway with each step. Dried dirt flew with every swing.

Malcolm carefully closed the door to the computer lab, then dug his camera out of his pants pocket.

"Oh, I get it," Dandy said.

Malcolm typed his school password into one of the computers, then connected the camera. It was no surprise when he checked the uploaded pictures.

In the first photo, the fisherman sat on top of the marquee. Today it had said: *Volleyball tryouts tonight! Go Hornets!* But *Tell No One!* had replaced *Go Hornets!* once again.

In the next photo, the fisherman was giving a droopy-eyed janitor bunny ears. The fisherman was grinning goofily, but the janitor had no idea. *Tell No One!* was now on the janitor's mop bucket.

In the library photo, he stood next to the 700 section. It seemed pretty fitting that he was in section where the "fishing for kids" books were shelved. He was holding up the book *Tell No One for Dummies.*

Malcolm wasn't surprised that every picture had the words TELL NO ONE! He just wished he knew what that meant.

"Malcolm, recess is almost over," Dandy whispered. "I'm way more scared of Mrs. Goolsby than of a ghost giving bunny ears. Can we go clean our shoes before the bell rings?"

Malcolm sighed. "Yeah, just give me another second." He printed out all three of the pictures and tucked them under his shirt. Then he and Dandy headed for the restroom to clean off their sneakers.

CHAPTER SEVEN

FISHING FOR ANSWERS

Malcolm dropped his load of school books on the kitchen table, then looked over his homework assignments. *Maybe I should transfer to military school*, he thought. *It'd be a lot easier.* He plopped himself down in a chair.

The house was particularly quiet. Dad was still at work. Mom and Cocoa were out shopping for more new school clothes—even though they'd bought Cocoa a closetful last weekend! Girls!

Grandma Eunice came walking in, pushing her wheelchair in front of her. Everyone else in the family thought she was weak and had lost her mind. Grandma played along so she could get out of doing household chores, but Malcolm knew the truth. It was their secret.

"Grandma, why do you even own that stupid wheelchair? I know you don't need it."

Grandma turned the chair toward the table. "Your mom thinks I'm too weak to walk on my own. But, I keep it so I'll always have a chair handy." She demonstrated by sitting down. Then she took a banana from the bowl and began peeling.

"Look at all this homework," Malcolm said. "My new teacher is tough."

Grandma Eunice clacked her false teeth around, getting ready for a bite. "That's nothing," she stated. "Back in my day . . ."

Here we go again! Malcolm thought.

". . . I had wake up at four A.M. to milk the cows before walking seven miles to school barefoot. The teacher would beat us with a rattlesnake if we were just five minutes tardy!"

"A rattlesnake?" Malcolm said, not believing it one bit.

"And we didn't have all those fancy computers and calculators. It was all done up here." She tapped the side of her head. A piece of yucky banana string stuck to her hair.

She went on, "You all whine and worry when

your computers won't boot up. We whined and worried when our pencils wore down. And we didn't have those gliding gel pens like your sister writes her love poems with."

Malcolm knew then that Grandma Eunice had been sneaking through Cocoa's things. It was about time, too. After all, she'd been borrowing his specter detector to find Grandpa Bertram all summer.

"We had fountain pens," she rumbled. "Fountain pens with inkwells. It was a mess! Splotchy papers . . . stained fingers and ink spots on your favorite clothes—"

"Yeah," Malcolm interrupted. "Those were the good old days."

"You're darn tooting!" Grandma said. She crammed the banana into her mouth and mushed down with her choppers.

Malcolm opened his science book. Science was his favorite subject— especially the current lesson on mapping the constellations.

He tried to concentrate, but his mind kept straying back to the mysterious fisherman. Plus, Grandma Eunice was making outrageously loud smacking noises with her teeth.

Malcolm looked up as she flung the banana peel over her shoulder, scoring a two-pointer as it hit the trash. He shook his head as she celebrated.

"Grandma," he started, "you're good at keeping secrets, right?"

Grandma Eunice shrugged. "Even if I told, who'd believe me?"

A good point, but still Malcolm hesitated. He wanted to show her the photos. He could use another opinion, but the messages clearly said *TELL NO ONE!* And if there was one thing Malcolm had learned in his lifetime, it was never take an exclamation point lightly. But then again . . .

"Does this have to do with your ghost hunting?" Grandma asked.

"Yeah," Malcolm said, sheepishly. He showed her the photos and updated her on what had happened so far. "Do you know him?"

Grandma shook her head. "No, I've never seen him before."

"Why do you think he keeps appearing if he doesn't want me to tell anyone?"

"You can't trust a fisherman, Malcolm. They'll make up a whopper of a fish tale without blinking. I remember once when Grandpa Bertram went fishing with some of his pals. Tried to convince me that he'd reeled up a barracuda, hopped on its back, and rode it like he was in the rodeo."

"And you didn't believe him?"

Grandma rolled her eyes. "That barracuda would be stuffed and hanging on the wall if it were true."

"So you think the ghost is making this up and really wants me to tell?" he asked, reaching up and plucking the banana string from her hair.

Grandma Eunice stared him straight in the eyes. "Maybe you should go ask him."

After thinking it over for about thirty seconds, Malcolm went to the phone and called Dandy. "We've got to go back to the school."

Dandy gasped. "Are you kidding me? Our weekly vocabulary list is longer than the dictionary, and I'm still trying to figure out how to connect the dots on these constellations."

"We can do our homework together later. Get your bike and meet me on the corner." Malcolm hung up and began gathering his supplies. He had fishing to do.

CHAPTER EIGHT
IN AND OUT

Malcolm tugged on the school's front door. Locked. There were lights on, and a few people milled about inside. Finally, a teacher came over and pushed open the door.

"What do you need?" she asked.

"I forgot my homework," Malcolm fibbed. He couldn't tell her the truth. How do you explain to a teacher that you really need to make contact with a ghostly fisherman to find out what it is he doesn't want you to tell? Much too complicated.

"In and out," the teacher said, holding the door open.

Malcolm and Dandy rushed by her, hurrying through the lobby and down the hall. They ducked into an empty classroom.

"What now?" Dandy wondered. "There are still teachers around."

Malcolm, busy digging his specter detector out of his backpack, said, "We'll just have to avoid them."

He flipped the switch to the On position. Someone passed by the doorway. The boys flattened themselves against the wall.

"Maybe we should've come at night," Dandy suggested. "When all the teachers were gone."

"That's when the janitors are here. No way they would let us in." Malcolm watched the warm-up light on his gadget, then flipped it to Detect.

Bleep, bleep, bleep, bleep, bleep!

It immediately picked up ghost activity.

The boys looked at each other and glanced around the empty classroom. Then . . .

Yip! Yip!

They both jumped with fright.

"Spooky!" Malcolm said softly. "You followed us?"

Yip! Yip! The dog happily bounced around like he was on springs.

"Go home," Malcolm ordered. "Now!"

Spooky, not the most obedient of ghost pets, raced in and out of Malcolm's feet. Literally!

"What are we going to do now?" Dandy asked.

"Good question," Malcolm said. "As long as Spooky's here the specter detector will bleep. We won't know if the fisherman is around until he actually appears."

"Yeah, and I don't want him sneaking up on me with a big old shark hook or something," Dandy added.

Spooky continued his hyper play.

"Settle down, boy," Malcolm warned. "We can't let anyone see you."

The boys stood, watching Spooky run in circles and yip at most everything.

"We've got to do something," Malcolm finally said. "The longer we stay here, the better our chances of getting caught."

Dandy rubbed his head in thought. "If there was just some way to distract him. Like with a Frisbee."

"Frisbees go right through him," Malcolm reminded Dandy.

"What we need is a ghost cat," Dandy said. "That would keep him busy."

Malcolm nodded. "Or another dog to distract him."

After a moment, Dandy lit up, giving Malcolm an award-winning grin. "I've got an idea." He pointed to the overhead projector.

Making sure no living person was lurking nearby, Malcolm and Dandy pulled the projector out of the corner and plugged it in. Dandy flipped the switch, causing a large lighted square to appear on the wall.

"Watch this," he said. Dandy moved his hands in front of the projector, making a doggie shadow puppet. He even added sound effects. "Yip! Yip!" he imitated.

That got Spooky's attention. *Yip! Yip!* he barked back.

"Keep him busy," Malcolm said. "I'll go see if I can find our ghost."

"Wait," Dandy called. "When you leave with the specter detector, Spooky will disappear. I won't be able to see him."

Malcolm looked at Spooky, who seemed to be smitten with Dandy's shadow dog. "As long as you keep that up, he'll be here. I'm going to go find our fisherman."

Making sure no one was in the hall, Malcolm slipped out. He aimed the ghost detector into the teachers' workroom. Nothing. Then he tried the boys' restroom. Still nothing. Then Malcolm did the bravest thing he'd ever done—he aimed it into the girls' restroom. Nothing there either.

Malcolm slowly made his way to the library. He passed Mrs. Goolsby's room. Strangely, she wasn't there. Malcolm had imagined that she stayed at school late into the night, working on massive piles of lesson plans. Mrs. Goolsby wasn't there. But someone else was.

In the corner by the American flag, stood the fisherman. On the classroom whiteboard he'd written *TELL NO ONE!* over and over, like a kid punished for doing something wrong.

Malcolm carefully approached. "H-h-hello," he muttered.

The fisherman turned toward him. He eyed Malcolm for a moment and then asked, "Can I trust you?"

Malcolm nodded. He wanted to say yes, but his throat felt cottony and dry. He didn't think he'd ever get used to being able to talk to ghosts. He just kept nodding his head.

"This is extremely important," the fisherman said.

Malcolm tried to sound brave. "Wh-wh-who are you?"

The fisherman pointed to the words he'd written on the whiteboard. "This is extremely important."

"Okay," Malcolm said.

The ghost took a step closer.

"I need—"

"Excuse me!"

Malcolm jumped. He whipped around at the voice. It was the teacher who'd let him in.

"I said in and out," she nagged. "Let's get a move on."

Malcolm glanced over his shoulder. The fisherman had disappeared. He shut off his detector and walked out. After rescuing Dandy, the boys hopped on their bikes and left empty-handed.

CHAPTER NINE

SOLVING ONE PROBLEM, CREATING ANOTHER

Malcolm couldn't concentrate on his homework. His mind kept drifting back to his brief encounter with the fisherman. Malcolm had learned two things.

1. Dandy can do an incredible shadow puppet.
2. The ghost at school had something extremely important to say.

He had to find out what. But once he found out, would he be able to tell anyone? *TELL NO ONE!* He went to bed, still pondering what he should do.

The next morning, Malcolm felt like a zombie. He stumbled through his morning routine, which consisted of eating his cereal while avoiding his sister. He had enough problems without listening to hers. He headed out to the bus in a daze.

Mrs. Goolsby's grating voice woke him with a jolt. "Class," she started, "I've been easy on you until now. But let's face it, summer vacation is over. We've had a couple of days to adjust. It's time to get back to work."

Malcolm glanced at Dandy, whose face had turned the color of plaster.

Mrs. Goolsby continued. "I expect the best from this class. That's why we're going to do some extra math drills this morning. Please pull out your textbooks and turn to the problems at the end of the chapter. We'll do a few on the board first. Then you'll do the rest on your own. And it will be timed!"

Dandy's face now turned whiter than any ghost they'd encountered.

"Let's start with the first problem. Malcolm, please come up and work it on the board."

Malcolm slipped out of his desk, carrying his math book. He looked at the whiteboard. It was mostly covered with schedules, lesson plans, and quiz dates.

Only one small section was left clean. That was the same section the fisherman had used to write his message. Malcolm slowly picked up a marker. If he snapped a picture of the whiteboard right now, would the messages appear on film? Probably.

He couldn't be concerned with that. He had a major math problem to solve right now. He could solve the ghost problem later.

Malcolm scribbled the problem on the board. *Five hundred and eighty people went to the mall on Saturday. Twice as many people went to the mall on Sunday. How many people went to the mall for the entire weekend?*

As he worked the problem, Malcolm couldn't help but think those 580 people were all clones of his sister, Cocoa, the Mall Queen!

He finished and faced Mrs. Goolsby. She addressed the class. "Do we all agree with Malcolm's answer?"

Most of the students nodded. A few gave a halfhearted, "Yes."

"You may take your seat," Mrs. Goolsby told him.

She didn't have to tell him twice. He grabbed his textbook and hurried back to his seat.

As he scooted by, something fell from the back of his math book and fluttered to the floor. Mrs. Goolsby bent down to retrieve it.

"You dropped this," she said, strolling over to Malcolm's desk. Just before handing it over, she looked at it. It was the picture Malcolm had taken of the fisherman by the marquee.

Mrs. Goolsby's mouth dropped open, her face went pale, and she fainted on the spot.

CHAPTER TEN

IDENTIFIED

After a huge commotion in the classroom, someone ran for help. Another teacher hurried in and helped Mrs. Goolsby up. She saw the picture again, then *bam!* fainted a second time. The nurse came in next and helped Mrs. Goolsby out of the room.

"I need to lie down," Mrs. Goolsby said, holding the back of her hand to her forehead. The nurse tucked the picture into her pocket to hide it from the teacher's view.

Malcolm waited. Minutes passed. The class sat quietly, as instructed, working the rest of the math problems. Malcolm held his pencil, pretending to work. He knew what was coming.

After minutes that felt like hours, a voice came over the speaker. "Malcolm Stewart please report to Mrs. Bergen's office." Mrs. Bergen . . . the principal!

Dandy gave Malcolm a "good luck" look as he walked out.

• • •

"Take a seat," Mrs. Bergen, instructed.

Malcolm sat.

Mrs. Bergen was holding the picture. She glanced at it, then at Malcolm, then back at the photo.

Malcolm wished Dandy was there to back him up. How on earth was he going to explain this? And even more important, why was Mrs. Bergen not rattled at seeing a ghost!

"I understand you're on the yearbook staff this year," Mrs. Bergen said, her voice steady.

"Yes," Malcolm answered.

He remembered his idea to swap Mrs. Bergen's head with the school mascot. Maybe he should scrap that plan.

"And you brought your camera to school for that reason?" she went on.

"Yes." *Gulp.* Malcolm's throat was so dry it felt like he was swallowing dust.

"While we appreciate your efforts," she droned, "I may have to call your parents about this."

Malcolm tried not to look as confused as he felt. Call his parents? Because he took a picture of a ghost?

"I'm aware of all the fancy trick photography programs for computers," she said. "But Malcolm, what you did to Mrs. Goolsby was a terrible joke. Do you understand that?"

Malcolm shook his head in confusion. He didn't understand anything!

"Now, I don't know how you found a photo of him. Frankly, I don't want to know. But putting her missing husband into a picture, then making sure she saw it—" She stopped speaking and clenched her fists as though to steady her words. "It's a prank of the cruelest sort."

What? Malcolm's brain tried to compute what he was hearing. *The fisherman was Mrs. Goolsby's husband?*

"B-but—," Malcolm sputtered.

Mrs. Bergen raised her palm up like a crossing guard demanding him to halt. "I don't want to hear it." She took a deep breath. "You owe Mrs. Goolsby an apology. Follow me."

Mrs. Bergen rose and motioned for Malcolm to follow. He trudged along behind her. A couple of quick turns led them into the school clinic.

Mrs. Goolsby was lying down holding the photo, an ice pack on her forehead.

Malcolm approached his teacher, his head down. "Mrs. Goolsby, I'm so sorry that picture upset you."

"I don't want an apology, Malcolm. I want

an explanation. My husband left for a fishing trip five years ago . . . just two days before our wedding anniversary. He never returned. How on earth did you get this picture of him?"

"Mrs. Goolsby," Malcolm began.

"And how did you know he called me Noonie?"

"Noonie?" Malcolm's head snapped up. He stared hard at Mrs. Goolsby. He had no idea what she meant.

"Yes. My husband called me Noonie. He nicknamed me that because we first met each other at the college diner right at noon. So, he always spelled it N-O-O-N-E."

TELL NO ONE! TELL NOONE!

Now Malcolm got it. "I promise, Mrs. Goolsby, I didn't tamper with that photo. That's how it came out."

He had no choice but to tell the truth. He hoped she'd believe him. "I think your husband is trying to tell you something."

Mrs. Goolsby glanced at the picture, then at Malcolm. She sat up, leaning closer to him.

"What do you think he's trying to tell me?" she whispered.

"I don't know. Let's find out," Malcolm whispered back.

CHAPTER ELEVEN

HAPPY ANNIVERSARY!

Malcolm went back to the classroom to retrieve his camera. The class was now being led by a substitute teacher.

"Excuse me," he interrupted, "I need Daniel to come with me." He held up the camera. "For official school business."

The sub nodded.

Dandy sheepishly got up from his desk. His face had turned a carsick green.

"I'm in trouble too?" Dandy asked when they reached the hall.

"No, but I may need you to back me up, in case things don't go as planned."

"What plan?" Dandy slowed his steps.

"Just come on," Malcolm said.

Dandy looked even sicker when he saw Mrs. Goolsby waiting for them.

"Follow me," Malcolm told them.

The three walked out the front door and over to the school's marquee. Malcolm took a quick picture. He checked the camera to make sure what he needed was there. "We'll be able to see it better after we upload it to a computer."

It didn't take long.

"It's the fisherman," Dandy said. "I thought we weren't supposed to tell. Why are we showing Mrs. Goolsby?"

Malcolm smiled. "Well, it turns out we were supposed to tell a certain Noone."

"Huh?" Dandy asked.

"I'll explain later," Malcolm said. "Now look closely. Do you see what I see?"

The photo clearly showed Mrs. Goolsby's husband pointing to the marquee. It now read: *Noone, I'm sorry I missed our anniversary. Check the pocket of my gray jacket. The one I wore when we were married.*

Mrs. Goolsby looked like she may faint a third time. Instead, she excused herself. "You boys go back to class. I think I'll go home for the day."

Malcolm took more pictures around school that afternoon. Mostly banners and bulletin boards, anything with writing on it. But they all came out just as they were originally written. No special messages. No fisherman.

The next morning, Malcolm and Dandy heard an odd noise coming from their classroom. They cautiously approached the door. The fisherman ghost may have been friendly before, but maybe he had more to say.

When they peeked around the door, they found Mrs. Goolsby humming! She wore a smile as bright as the gleaming diamond necklace around her neck. She brightened even more when she saw Malcolm.

"Malcolm, may I speak to you for a moment?" she asked him.

Malcolm glanced at Dandy. Then he approached Mrs. Goolsby's desk.

"Thank you," she whispered, pointing to the necklace. "I found it in my husband's jacket pocket, along with a lovely anniversary card."

Malcolm wasn't sure exactly what to say. "It's pretty."

"Yes . . . yes, it is," she agreed. "I'll never know what happened to my husband, but at least now I know he loved me. I have you to thank for that."

Malcolm blushed. Then Mrs. Goolsby let him go back to his desk. He dug in his desk for his math book to get ready for more punishing days of problems.

Malcolm waited for the ruler to snap the class to attention, but that day Mrs. Goolsby waited until after the announcements to begin the lessons.

"I think rather than doing problems," she began, "today we'll begin with a math game."

"A game?" Dandy dared to ask.

"Yes," Mrs. Goolsby answered, all smiles. "Learning doesn't always have to be hard work."

Malcolm pulled out some paper and a pencil. *What a difference a ghost can make,* he thought. Maybe it would be a great school year after all.

TOP FIFTEEN WAYS TO DETECT A GHOST, SPIRIT, OR POLTERGEIST

From Ghost Detectors Malcolm and Dandy

1. Check for creepy surroundings. Is there a graveyard nearby? Or an area covered in strange shadows? Is there a house that stares at you?
2. Ask people if there are stories about the area. Is there a legend about a haunting? Has anyone else seen a spirit there?
3. Listen to the area at night. Do you hear moaning, whispering, or laughter that doesn't belong?
4. Cautiously enter the area. Does the porch creak? Are there cobwebs all around?
5. Turn on your specter detector and wait for the *bleep*. Just be sure to keep close to the wall and try not to trip on your shoelaces!

You never know what will be around the next corner!

6. Ghosts often hide out in empty houses. If you are watching a neighbor's house, check the windows before getting too close.

7. Seeing transparent people in dark windows is a definite sign of ghosts.

8. Remember that dogs are more sensitive to ghosts than people. Watch your dog to see if it barks at thin air.

9. Ghosts can also give off a disgusting smell. Is there a smell of rotting onions mixed with feet nearby?

10. Not all ghosts are mean. If you find stray bags of jellybeans lying around, they may be a gift from a relative. Just in case though, turn on your specter detector and wait for the bleep!

11. Spirits can be found anywhere. So, be on the lookout for ghosts everywhere you go. Keep your ghost detector handy at all times.

12. Ghost hunters often use electronic devices to find ghosts. Use your camera or a recording device to search for spirits.

13. Take Polaroids and digital photos to get quick pictures of spirits.
14. Carefully check your pictures for bright spots called orbs. Some people think these spots show poltergeists.
15. Like Mr. Goolsby, some ghosts are trying to send a message. Just in case, turn on your specter detector and wait for the bleep! When the ghost appears, don't be afraid to say hi!

Dotti Enderle was born in Killeen, Texas, and despite being labeled a "reluctant reader" as a child, grew up to write and publish dozens of books for children, including *Grandpa for Sale* and *The Library Gingerbread Man*. Storytelling is in her blood, and she has entertained at numerous schools, libraries, museums, and festivals since 1993. She takes pride in her vast collection of original stories and folk tales, and specializes in participation stories, which allow her audience to join in the fun. Today, you'll find her reading, writing, and smiling in Houston, Texas.

Howard McWilliam left his day job as a financial journalist and editor in late 2005 to pursue his love of illustrating. Now, he illustrates regularly for a wide range of magazines and newspapers, including *The Daily Telegraph* and *The Week*. He branched into illustrating children's books in 2009 and has illustrated multiple titles including *I Need My Monster*, *When a Dragon Moves In*, the Alfie the Werewolf series, and more. He lives in Kingston upon Thames, England, with his wife, Rebecca.